FALLING FAST

DEA FAST SERIES

KAYLEA CROSS

D1512137

FALLING FAST

Copyright © 2017
by Kaylea Cross

* * * * *

Cover Art & Formatting by
Sweet 'N Spicy Designs

* * * * *

ISBN: 978-1542618700

Dedication

For Katie Reus, my sister-from-another-mother, for always being in my corner and lending a helping hand when the going gets tough.

Love you bunches. xo

Author's Note

Dear readers,

This book marks the start of my DEA FAST series, featuring the men of FAST Bravo and the ladies who win their hearts. *Falling Fast* picks up right at the end of Easton's Claim, and continues Charlie and Jamie's story. I hope you enjoy it and fall in love with this new band of brothers I'm about to introduce you to.

Happy reading!

Kaylea Cross

Chapter One

Sugar Hollow, VA
September

Rifle clutched tight in her hands, Charlie ran through the dense tangle of trees that bordered the perimeter of her family's property. She'd been hunting on this land since she was a little girl, but never like this.

This time, her prey was human.

Her target was somewhere ahead of her, likely trying to escape to the road. She slapped a branch aside and jumped over a log, the thin moonlight casting sinister shadows along the path she was on.

The man was hidden by the forest and its thick underbrush. He and his thug teammates had come here and threatened her family tonight. The smell of smoke hung in the air from when the men had set the barn on fire with her and the others inside it, then shot at them. Thank God none of her family members had been hit.

His entire team was already dead or in custody, and he was next.

Charlie ran faster, anger coursing through her veins with every step. She knew every inch of this land, every secret path and shortcut. Her enemy didn't.

The soles of her boots were quiet against the thick carpet of freshly fallen leaves. Even as she ran she was aware of the man behind her, following her through the woods. Special Agent Jamie Rodriguez, DEA Foreign-Deployed Advisory and Support Team member, teammate of her brother, Easton. The man who'd lit her body up with a few sizzling kisses a couple months ago, then cut contact.

Personal history aside, having him at her back now gave her an added measure of confidence. She trusted him and his training. Whatever happened out here, he'd have her back.

Up ahead she caught a glimpse of movement in the shadows. A man's silhouette flashed between two trees, then was swallowed up again by the darkness.

She jerked to a halt and crouched down, bringing her rifle to her shoulder. The wooden stock was cool against her cheek. Again she caught a flash of movement but didn't have a clear shot. She'd have to move closer.

Standing, she backtracked a few paces and took another trail that veered out toward the road. "Psst, over here," Charlie called out to Jamie in a loud whisper that carried through the darkness.

She darted away before he could answer and stopped behind a stand of trees, using the gnarled trunks as cover. Glancing over her shoulder, she searched for Jamie, spotted him about twenty yards behind her. "I see him. He's heading for the road," she whispered again, loud as she dared.

"Stay there and don't move," he ordered, his low voice cutting through the quiet.

No way. She wasn't letting this asshole get to the road and possibly make it to a getaway vehicle. She ignored the command and kept going, scanning for the shooter up ahead.

There.

Charlie dropped to one knee and brought her weapon up. Aimed at his center mass, the countless hours at shooting ranges making the movement automatic.

But the shooter must have either sensed or heard her, because he whirled and aimed right at her.

For one terrible instant, her heart seized as icy fear slid through her. The blood rushed in her ears as she stared at her target and squeezed the trigger, firing two shots in rapid succession.

The man grunted and hit the ground with a solid thud. She stayed put for a few tense seconds, waiting to see if he moved, but then the thud of sprinting footsteps sounded just behind her.

Shock punched through her as she stared at the man she'd just shot.

An instant later Jamie flew past her and ran straight for the fallen man, his own weapon up. She got up and followed on unsteady legs, vividly aware that she'd just stared death in the face and shot a human being.

The guy was on his back, groaning, unmoving. Blood glistened darkly on his chest, streamed out of his mouth and nose. She'd shot him through the lung. She swallowed, told herself she had nothing to feel bad about.

Without pause Jamie kicked the dying man's rifle out of reach and knelt to search him. The man's groans stopped and he lay there with his eyes half-open, staring at her sightlessly. Jamie pulled a wallet and a backup weapon off him, then placed two fingers beneath the angle of the man's jaw.

Charlie's heart thudded against her sternum. "Is he dead?" She already knew the answer, but she needed to hear the word.

"Yeah." Pushing to his feet, he slid the wallet into the front pocket of his jeans and turned to stand between her and the body so she wouldn't have to see it.

Too late. The dead man's face and that blank stare were already burned into her brain.

She held tight to the rifle in her hands, tried not to panic as anxiety swirled in her stomach. Jamie had witnessed what happened. She hadn't meant to kill the guy, just incapacitate him.

He would have shot you if you hadn't fired first. It was self-defense.

The panic ebbed a little. Surely the investigators would believe her. She had Jamie to corroborate her version of events, and the evidence would prove her story.

"Come on," Jamie said in a low voice, reaching out to catch one of her hands.

She blinked and looked at his face for the first time since they'd headed out here. The thin moonlight glinted off his short, dark hair, highlighted the dark stubble on his jaw. He pulled her along with him, rubbed his thumb over her fingers to help warm them.

She followed without a word, mind spinning.

As he led her back through the woods toward the pasture, he pulled out his cell to call Easton and let him know the last shooter was down, and that they were about to emerge from the trees onto the western pasture.

When the old yellow farmhouse came into view at last, sheer relief hit her. The barn stood nearby, the smell of smoke thick in the air but at least the fire was out. More than ever, she needed to be surrounded by the comfort of her family right now.

The back lawn was already swarming with cops, Feds in marked windbreakers and firefighters in their turnout gear. The investigators would want to question her, take her fingerprints. Charlie lifted her chin and kept walking. She hadn't done anything wrong, had nothing to hide.

Jamie stopped suddenly and turned to face her, his face an unreadable mask in the faint light. "You okay?" he murmured.

"Fine." It came out much more curt than she'd intended. But she didn't want him to know how unsteady she felt inside. That killing a man, even in self-defense, had shaken her.

He sighed, looking frustrated. "He would have shot you if you hadn't pulled the trigger."

She nodded, jaw tight. "I know." A tremor snaked through her at the reminder.

Without a word, he tugged her close and wrapped his arms around her. Hard. She was stiff at first, but when all he did was hold her, she relaxed. "Cold?" he murmured.

"A little." God, he felt good. Solid, warm, strong. She closed her eyes and rested her cheek on his shoulder, drawing strength from him. She was so damn glad he'd been out here with her tonight. In hindsight, she realized she should have listened to him when he'd ordered her to stay put.

He held her in silence for a few minutes, running his hands up and down her back, keeping her tight to his chest. His clean, masculine scent and the feel of those strong arms around her helped calm her, center her.

At last he squeezed her and pressed a kiss to the top of her head. For some reason that kiss put a lump in her throat. "Better?" he asked.

She nodded, not trusting her voice. This man stirred something inside her that no one else had and she didn't want him to see how vulnerable she was at that moment. Not when it might give him the upper hand in this sensual power struggle they were engaged in.

Lowering his arms, he eased back a few inches to stare down at her in the wash of light coming through the back windows of the main house. "You're trouble," he said.

What?

She lifted her gaze to meet his, anger surging through her as she stared into those honey-brown eyes. They had set out together to deal with the final shooter, and she'd done what was necessary to eliminate the threat. "They attacked my home, my family. Was I just supposed to sit on my ass and wring my hands while you guys handled it alone?"

Annoyance burned in his eyes. "No, but I didn't expect you to run for the nearest rifle and chase after the shooter, either."

Then what the hell had he expected her to do? "I was backing you up." Okay, so she didn't have his tactical expertise, but he didn't know the land like she did. She'd just followed her instincts. She'd taken that trail because it would give them an advantage. Without her, they might have lost the guy.

Yeah, and you're lucky you're still breathing right now.

She pushed aside a subconscious shiver at the thought and continued glaring up at Jamie.

"No, you took off on your own and put yourself in danger. That's not how teammates back each other up."

Her eyes widened at the verbal slap. Compared to the vulnerability of a minute ago, this shot of annoyance felt damn good. She might be a Computer Forensic Examiner for the DEA, not a field agent, but she was far from helpless. "Just because I'm a woman doesn't mean I'm weak or defenseless. You think that just because of my gender and occupation, I don't know how to handle a weapon? I was raised in a household of four Marines, and even if I didn't serve like they did, I still shoot like a Marine."

To her surprise, he seemed to fight back a smile. "Yeah, you sure as hell do."

She blinked at the abrupt change in his demeanor and eyed him in suspicion. "That's right." She might be a civilian, but she was far from helpless. And she didn't want him to think she was weak.

He stared down at her for another moment, searching her eyes. "Remind me never to piss you off."

She narrowed her eyes at him. "Too late."

He smothered a laugh, but she didn't see any of this as funny. It had been a bitch of a night so far, and he wasn't making it any better. She'd rather he'd just hugged her and kept his damn mouth shut.

Before she could decide whether to blast him or spin around and head for the house, he took her completely off guard by cupping the back of her head with one hand and bringing his mouth down on hers. She sucked in a swift breath and put her free hand on his chest, ready to shove him away.

Jamie wrapped his free arm around her waist and hauled her tighter up against him, his quiet groan setting off a burst of heat low in her abdomen. The kiss was urgent, needy, making her mind go blank as pleasure speared her.

He'd kissed her before, but this was the first time he'd been the aggressor.

That night back in April outside the club, he'd merely followed her cues and given her a taste of what she'd wanted while pinning her up against the brick wall outside. But she'd sensed far more in him.

An unyielding dominance that he'd kept ruthlessly chained. The opposite of her usual type, yet for some reason she found it insanely sexy on him. He was a challenge she hadn't been able to ignore. Still was.

And she'd thought far too much about pushing him to the breaking point over the past few months.

Now he was the one in control, and this was more than a kiss—he was staking a claim. And Charlie thrilled in it, the strong, independent part of her be damned. She didn't even care that he was making out with her on the lawn within sight of the house. Everyone was too preoccupied to even notice them.

More sirens sounded to the west, where they'd just come from, breaking the spell. He broke the kiss and stared down at her in the dimness, the raw heat in his eyes stealing her breath. He looked at her like he wanted to eat her up.

"Cavalry's finally here," he murmured, breaking the seething physical tension, and rubbed his thumb over her cheek.

She straightened and licked her lips, a little smile tugging at the corners of her mouth to make it seem like she wasn't still reeling from that kiss. That he hadn't just tilted her world on its axis. It felt like she'd just ridden a damn rollercoaster. "Late as usual."

"Mmm," he agreed, and dipped his head to kiss her again. Softer this time, a tender brush of his lips over hers. Making something flip low in her belly. She'd wondered far too much about what he'd be like in bed. These two sides of him, forceful and tender, would be a lethal combination if used together. "Let's get back to the house before they come looking for us."

The moment Charlie walked into the house, her father and two of her brothers were there to hug her. Then the questioning began. The Feds split everyone up to get their individual stories while other agents and local cops searched the property. One agent took Charlie into the dining room to talk to her alone.

"The man who ordered the attack," he began when they were settled at the large farmhouse table. "You know him?"

"No, but I know his name. Brandon Gallant." Now in custody. Her brothers had tracked him down and cornered him. "He's a drug dealer who had a vendetta against our friend Piper's ex."

He nodded. "Greg Rutland."

"Yes." Who was now dead, killed by either Gallant or one of his men. "Gallant wanted money and information that Greg apparently stole from him. Greg hid cash and a flash drive in some old furniture Piper stored out in our shed. We think Greg kept it as collateral, for protection from Gallant." Little good it had done him.

The agent wrote it all down. "Tell me about the man you and agent Rodriguez chased through the woods."

Charlie took a deep breath. As she answered, cold began to seep into her again. She wrapped her arms around her middle and curled up tighter in her chair as she recounted those final moments that had ended with her pulling the trigger. The dead man's face was crystal clear in her mind.

"You want a blanket?" he asked her, noting how she'd started to shiver.

"No, I'm fine. It's just...I've never had to do anything like that before." And she never wanted to have to take a life again. She didn't know how her dad and brothers handled it.

"I understand. I'll make this as quick as I can."

"The threat to my family. Is it over now?" That was the most important thing to her.

He met her eyes, paused a moment. "It'll be a few days before we can get a better handle on that. But with Gallant in custody and the flash drive and money turned over to us, the direct threat to all of you has been eliminated."

But whoever Gallant had worked for was still out there. As well as the rest of the cartel.

She shelved that thought and focused on the rest of the questions. By the time they were done, it was two in the morning and Charlie was having serious fantasies about falling into her bed upstairs.

Too bad Jamie wouldn't be with her.

Exhausted, she flopped down on the couch in the living room and rested her head on her father's shoulder with a sigh. She wasn't in any trouble for killing the shooter but she couldn't get his face out of her head. Those staring eyes.

Movement in her peripheral vision brought her head up a moment later. Jamie, heading for the front door with his duffel in hand.

Walking out without even saying goodbye after everything—after the way he'd kissed her earlier?

Oh no you're not. Not this time.

He was almost to the door when Charlie called out to him. "You leaving?" she asked, stepping around the corner into the hallway so they had privacy.

He stopped, turned to face her, his face unreadable. No trace of guilt at all, or the heat she'd seen and felt from him earlier. "Yeah."

She frowned, trying to figure him out. "So you were just going to leave without saying goodbye?" It was totally shitty of him to sneak out on her after everything that had happened tonight. She didn't care if he was trying to keep her at arm's length because her dad and two brothers were present. It was wrong.

He lifted a shoulder in an indifferent shrug. "You were busy with your family and I didn't want to take you away from them."

She hadn't pegged him as the kind of guy to make excuses and she was way too tired to pretend she wasn't annoyed by having to guess at whatever game he was playing. "Were you going to call me at least?"

"Yeah, I was. I need to go now, though." He turned to leave.

"Wait," she exclaimed, and rushed over to him. He stopped again, seemed to tense as she drew near, those warm amber eyes locked with hers. She halted a foot away from him and put her hands on her hips, his vitality and their unresolved sexual tension crackling in the air between them. Impossible to ignore. "When will I see you again?"

"Depends."

She lifted an eyebrow at the cryptic comment. "On?"

"On what you're willing to give. Because if you want to see me again, there's something you should know."

Well, this should be enlightening.

She folded her arms across her chest, deliberately bringing his gaze to her breasts, and cocked an eyebrow. His lips quirked in acknowledgment. "And what's that?" she asked, the edge of a taunt in her voice. She was no man's toy and refused to let him think he had the upper hand here. He wanted her every bit as badly as she wanted him, so as far as she was concerned, that put them on an even playing field.

He stared into her eyes for another long moment, all that formidable control and leashed male power making her shiver inside. "I play for keeps."

Charlie stared at him a moment, hardly able to believe her ears. What the hell was he talking about, playing for keeps? They barely *knew* each other, and she wasn't about to dive into a serious relationship with him just because he demanded it.

Before she could think of a decent comeback he leaned down to brush his lips across her cheek. "See you later, Trouble," he murmured. "Say goodbye to your family for me."

Then he picked up his bag and walked out into the cold night air, leaving her staring after him with a strange ache building in the center of her chest.

Chapter Two

Arlington, VA
Seven months later

Jamie bit back a wince as he pulled his body armor over his head and hung it up in his locker. It seemed like every muscle in his back, arms and shoulders were on fire.

"Dude, you gotta try this massage therapist I've been going to the past few weeks. She's little, but strong, and her hands..." Kai rolled his eyes heavenward before looking at him again. "I come outta there feeling amazing every time."

He shot his teammate a wry look. "I'm not into those kinds of places, thanks."

Kai's black eyebrows crashed together in a mock scowl, the swirling black tribal tats on his bare chest and shoulder rippling as he ran a hand through his short hair. He was half-Samoan with a lot of other Pacific Islander blood in him, and the biggest guy on the team—tall *and* stacked. Dude looked like he could bench press a small

Volkswagen if he felt like it. "It's not like that. It's totally legit. *Medical*. Covered by our extended health."

"I'm happy for you, man. Think I'll stick to a shower and then a soak in the hot tub for now though, thanks."

"I'm down with that," his best friend Easton said from beside him, peeling his sweat-soaked T-shirt off. "Damn, I'm wiped."

No surprise, after the day they'd put in. Two hours of PT, followed by four hours of rappelling practice, topped off with a five-mile run in full tac gear. Just part of the conditioning routine he and his FAST Bravo brothers had to maintain to stay at peak physical performance now that they were back stateside again. Different from his days back in the Army, but the aches and pains were the same.

Jamie took his cell phone from the shelf in his locker and checked it, smiled when he saw the message there.

"Hot date?" Kai asked from behind him, trying to peek over his shoulder.

Always so nosy. But the only woman Jamie wanted was off-limits, and had been for the past year. Another reason why he never should have kissed her again that night last fall. "My mom," he said, holding up the phone so Kai could see the text she'd sent.

How's my favorite son?

"Oh." Losing the joking demeanor, Kai stepped back and began rummaging in his locker. "How's she doing this week?"

His whole team knew the situation, and that he'd just been out to California to visit her last weekend. "The same," he said, typing back a response. *I'm good. Long day. Did you get a milkshake down you like I asked?* At least she was no worse. For now, anyway.

Kai nodded and opened his mouth to say something else, but faltered and went back to rummaging as though he didn't know what to say. Jamie understood. What was there to say?

His phone buzzed with a text. *Yes, half of one. Your father keeps trying to make me finish it.*

A sharp burst of pain lanced through his chest. *You can do it. Just about to hit the shower. Will call in a bit.* He needed a few minutes to collect himself before he talked to her. Every time he talked to her, he worried it would be the last time he heard her voice. And every time he went back home, it tore him in two when he left.

Setting the phone back on the shelf, he pushed out a sigh and looked over at Easton. His buddy was studiously gathering a change of clothes, not looking at him. Easton knew the score, knew exactly what Jamie was going through. It helped. "Wanna grab a burger before we head home?"

"Yeah, sounds good. Lend me your shaving kit, will ya?"

"Uh-uh, not until I'm done with it," Jamie answered, heading for the showers.

Scrubbed, refreshed and dressed in clean civvies, he strode back into the locker room where the seven other guys were grabbing their jackets and keys. "Colebrook and I are gonna grab a burger and a couple beers if anyone else wants in."

"I'm totally in," Kai said, stuffing his wallet in the back pocket of his jeans. His response surprised no one in the room, since he had the most voracious appetite of all of them and never turned down an opportunity to eat. The guy was an eating *machine*.

"Sorry boys, it'll have to wait."

Jamie swung around to face the doorway at the sound of that familiar voice. Their team leader, Supervisory Special Agent Brock Hamilton stood there, still dressed in the black T-shirt and camo utility pants he'd worn all day. "Rodriguez and Colebrook, I need a word."

Jamie exchanged a puzzled glance with Easton and

followed. "Meet you at the usual place after we're done here," he said to Kai on the way past.

Hamilton was already in his office, seated behind his wide desk when Jamie and Easton arrived. "Shut the door," he said.

Jamie pulled it shut and took a seat in one of the chairs in front of the desk as Easton took the other. This was unusual. "What's up?"

Hamilton pushed a manila folder across the desk at them and flipped it open, exposing a picture of an unfamiliar middle-aged blond man. "After a few months in max security prison, Brandon Gallant has had a change of heart and decided to cooperate with authorities."

The asshole drug trafficker responsible for the chaos at the Colebrook place back in September. Jamie had thought Gallant's arrest would be the end of that whole situation, but he'd been wrong. So what now? Something to do with the cartel he'd worked for?

"Apparently he just gave up some juicy intel on this guy," Hamilton went on, tapping the photo, "in exchange for a reduced sentence."

Jamie looked down at the open file, read the name. "Dean Baker." He glanced over at Easton. "Mean anything to you?"

"No. Who is he?" Easton asked Hamilton.

"We're gonna find out soon enough, because the three of us have a meeting to get to right now." His gunmetal-gray eyes slid to Easton. "And just so you're aware, the taskforce is calling in your sister too."

****

"You're gonna make me wear a pink dress, aren't you?" Charlie muttered as she looked over the dress images Piper had pulled up on the laptop before them. Her longtime friend was marrying Easton, the youngest of

Charlie's brothers.

"As the maid of honor, I'm letting you pick whatever color you want. And just for the record, with your dark hair and pale complexion, you would look adorable in pink."

Charlie made a face. "I hate adorable. Ravishing, powerful and sexy I can get behind, but not adorable."

Piper laid her head on Charlie's shoulder, her honey-blond hair spilling down the front of Charlie's bright red top. "Sorry, you're seven years younger than me, so you'll always be adorable to me."

Because it was Piper, Charlie wasn't annoyed. The woman was impossible not to love. She studied the bridesmaids dress choices before her with resigned distaste. Two had all kinds of girly ruffles that made her want to gag, but the third wasn't so bad. "You know I was a tomboy until I was eighteen, right?"

"Oh, I remember it well. And even when you decided to finally embrace your femininity, the boys were still too terrified of you to ask you out."

She snorted. "You mean they were too terrified of my dad and three overprotective older brothers."

"Well, them too." Piper sat up and gestured impatiently at the screen. "So? Can you stomach any of these?"

"This one's not bad," she said, pointing to the third one. The wedding was still a solid six months away, so there was no huge rush but by now she was more than used to Piper's penchant for being ultra-organized and ahead of the game. "What's Austen wearing?" Her eldest brother Wyatt's soon-to-be wife was the other bridesmaid.

In fact, all the Colebrook siblings except Charlie were getting married this year, and she was just fine with that. As the youngest sibling and only girl raised in an overprotective household of military alpha males, she was too busy savoring her freedom and independence since finally moving out on her own a couple years ago and had no plans to settle down anytime soon.

"Whichever she likes of the remaining two dresses, but as maid of honor you get first pick. Now come on."

"What about this one in a vivid blue?" Charlie tapped the third dress.

"Done." Beaming, Piper shot off a quick email to the dress boutique owner, then faced Charlie again. "Okay, let's talk bachelorette party. I don't want it to be a big shindig or anything. And I don't want to go clubbing all night, either."

That was just plain wrong. "Please, it's your last celebration as a single woman. You have to go clubbing. It's a rule."

Now Piper was the one who made a face. "All right, one club. But no sewing candies all over my shirt for strange guys to suck off me. Eww. And before the club, something more relaxing. A massage and pedicure or something like that, then a nice dinner together, with wine."

"You didn't always used to be this boring," Charlie teased with a grin.

"Ha, well I've had more than my share of excitement in the form of ridiculous, reality-show-worthy drama over the past few years. So trust me, I love being boring. Boring's where it's at."

Her grin faded. She hadn't meant to make Piper think of all that again. "I know you have. And you know I love you no matter what, and that I've always got your back." Piper had dealt with everything really well and had seemed to bounce back to her old self after burying her ex-husband. Easton was really proud of her.

Piper's whole face softened as she smiled. "Yes, and I love you too. I always wanted you to be my real sister, and now you finally will be."

"You were always like a sister to me." Piper had been part of the family since Charlie was a kid. "You marrying Easton just makes it official." But enough of this mushy stuff for the time being, because it was starting to make her squirmy. "So, what else is there to decide on today?"

"Tabs three through seven," Piper answered, patting the organized binder she'd set next to the laptop.

Charlie suppressed a groan. She'd taken a rare day off to go over all the wedding stuff with Piper because Piper had the day off from her teaching job. "Can we grab dinner first? I'm starving."

"Yes, totally. Let's go." She shut the laptop and got up.

As Charlie followed Piper to the door, her cell rang. Pulling it from her purse, she saw her boss's number.

For a moment she nearly answered, then thought better of it. She never took time off and if she answered now, he'd just call her in about something and she didn't feel like pulling an all-nighter. So she hit mute and tucked the phone back into her purse. Whatever he wanted could wait until she got back into the office tomorrow morning.

They'd no sooner stepped into the hallway than her phone vibrated. This time it was Easton calling. And the new voicemail showing on screen had to be from her boss.

"Nope, sorry. Busy," she murmured to her brother, feeling only a twinge of guilt as she shoved it back into her purse. Of all her brothers, she was closest to Easton, maybe because they were nearest in age.

That still wasn't enough reason to make her want to talk to him right now, even if he'd just gotten back from another four-month-long rotation in Afghanistan with his team.

Two steps from the elevator at the end of the hall, Piper's phone rang. Her face lit up when she looked at the screen. "It's Easton. Hey, handsome," she answered, all smiles.

Charlie waved her hands to get Piper's attention, whispering, "If he asks, don't tell him I'm—"

"Yeah, she's right here. You wanna talk to her?"

Charlie huffed out a sigh and leveled a hard look at Piper. "Seriously?" she muttered, taking the phone Piper offered. "My one day off in forever, and suddenly everybody wants a piece of me." She put the phone to her ear. "Hi."

"Something important just came up at work." Easton's uncharacteristically serious tone jarred her. "You need to come in for a meeting right away. How soon can you be at headquarters?"

A burst of alarm hit her. Nothing like this had ever happened in the two-plus years she'd been with the DEA. "Why, what's going on?"

"Can't say over the phone. So, how soon?"

Had to be important, for them to call her in like this. Her gut said it must be something to do with the undercover case her boss had spoken to her about the other day. "I'll be there in half an hour."

"Okay. See you soon. Give Piper a hug from me."

"I will."

Piper watched her with worried hazel-green eyes as Charlie ended the call. "What's happening?" she asked.

"Not sure, but I need to get to a meeting. Sorry." Charlie hugged her. "That's from Easton. We'll do lunch on the weekend maybe, yeah?"

"Sure. Tell him to call me so I know nothing's wrong, okay?"

"Sure."

Half an hour later she walked into DEA headquarters in Springfield, and headed up to the boardroom on her boss's floor. At her knock, he called out for her to enter, and when she pushed the door open, she was surprised at all the people already seated around the long table with him.

Her brother, his boss, and a Fed to his left she recognized from her family's place back in September during the aftermath of the Gallant manhunt. To her boss's right sat Taylor, a female agent from the organized crime division, as well as a close friend of Charlie's.

And, at the far end, Special Agent Jamie Rodriguez.

Their gazes locked for an instant, just long enough for a jolt of awareness and nerves to spear through her belly. What was he doing here?

Jerking her gaze away from him, she faced her boss. "Hi," she said, heading for the chair they'd left vacant for her at the center of the table, where a pen and pad of paper were waiting.

"Thanks for coming in on such short notice," he said. "Sorry for springing this on you like this. I would have talked to you about it privately first, but given what we've just found out, we've got a short window to move on this new intel." He gestured to the others seated around the table. "This is part of the taskforce we've assembled. We've been going over some new information on the Gallant case you need to be aware of."

The asshole who had been shot and arrested for attacking her family, and was currently wasting away in a maximum security prison. Or at least, she hoped he was wasting away. "All right." She sat down and folded her hands on top of the pad of paper, giving him her full attention and trying to ignore the weight of Jamie's stare from the end of the table. She'd made up her mind months ago to try and forget him. Not that it had worked out so well.

"Based on the information you and your team were able to gather from the flash drive your brother found last September, we were able to further interrogate Gallant about a few things. Until now he's been totally uncooperative, but his latest appeal just got denied, so he was willing to talk. He gave us some intel and a name to investigate, one already on our radar, in exchange for a reduction in his sentence."

Charlie kept her face impassive to hide her disgust. Brandon Gallant was a low-level drug trafficker wannabe, and a waste of skin. He was solely responsible for Piper's ex's death. Even if Charlie had loathed Greg Rutland for what he'd put Piper through over the last years of their marriage, he'd tried to protect Piper that night and hadn't deserved to die. "What's the name?"

"Dean Baker."

She recognized it as one she'd recovered from the flash drive once she and her team had cracked the encryption on the files and begun to delve through the information on it. Greg had sure dug up a lot of dirt on a lot of dirty people. Too bad that kind of leverage hadn't gained him any protection. "How is he connected to Gallant?"

"One of his most faithful business clients. On paper, Baker's totally clean, but he's a big-time money launderer. We just haven't been able to find any concrete dirt on him so far. That's our current problem, even though we have intel suggesting he's involved with a network of narcos. And that's also why we called you in for this meeting." He paused a beat, watching her expectantly, and she was aware of everyone staring at her. "We want you to sign on for a short undercover job for us."

Surprise flashed through her, but she managed to hide it. "Undercover?" He'd mentioned it to her in passing several weeks ago, that they were working on an undercover op to try and crack a cartel, setting up fake identities in preparation for it. As a civilian analyst, she'd never done anything like that before. Didn't have the specific training for it and didn't want it, because she loved her job and had no interest in becoming a field agent.

Her boss nodded. "According to Gallant, Baker is so clean on the surface that we can hunt all we want but won't find anything to incriminate him. He's meticulous, has managed to bury all his criminal activity thus far. Gallant says the only way to get what we need is to access the files on his personal laptop, which he keeps with him in a safe wherever he's staying. Right now, that's his vacation house in The Hamptons. The laptop is so heavily encrypted that we haven't been able to hack into it, and he hardly ever has it online."

Nodding, she filed all that away, more curious about the details of the undercover op than Baker's computer skills or security. "So you want me to get into his house and steal the files?" Because she had no earthly idea how that was going to work.

"Make a copy of them," he corrected. "His men will confiscate your phone and sweep you for bugs before you even get through the front door. You'll have to use the transmitting device the NSA gave us, figure out a way to hide it in an ordinary object that won't draw suspicion. It can remotely access a computer's files, copy them, then wirelessly transfer them to a remote terminal. Right?"

Well yeah, in theory. The transmitter was designed to be hidden in plain sight so that field operatives could use it during a sting without risk of detection. "As long as the computer's on and I can get within three feet of it, and provided I have some kind of wireless connection to send the files out with, then yes, it should work." Again, theoretically speaking. She hadn't personally tested it, because why would she, as an analyst?

"Good." He glanced to his left toward the end of the table before focusing back on her. "I assume you know SSA Brock Hamilton?"

Her brother's FAST team leader. She aimed a polite smile at the big, early-forty-something man with light brown hair seated next to Easton. "We've met briefly a couple of times before, yes." Hamilton returned the smile and nodded at her, his steel gray eyes warming.

"FAST Bravo is on standby during their training period for the next few months. We're aware that you're a civilian, and because of that, SSA Hamilton has given the green light for one of his men to be assigned to the op as personal protection for you. Your brother was the obvious choice but there's too much of a conflict of interest, so you'll be working with SA Rodriguez during this assignment instead, since you two already know each other."

Shock burst in her veins. Work undercover with Jamie? No way. A million arguments sprang to mind, so she blurted out the most obvious one. "But I'm not trained for it." It was so obvious, but under the circumstances, she felt the need to say it. She glanced at Taylor, and her friend seemed to be holding her breath.

"You don't need to be if Rodriguez is with you," her boss went on. "I know you can handle the specifics of the op, and you won't have a problem adapting to a cover identity once we train you up a little. Besides, given your upbringing, you're already better trained with a weapon than ninety-five percent of our civilian analysts. SSA Hamilton and I chose Rodriguez specifically because of your history with each other."

Uh, no you didn't. Because if they knew the true history between her and Jamie—and not just what happened after the attack last September—they never would have paired them together.

They'd met at a popular nightclub on a warm night last April. A few daiquiris with her girlfriends. Sultry music. Dancing with a tall, sexy stranger who'd caught her eye from across the room. Winding her arms around that sturdy neck, his hard chest and thighs brushing against hers as they swayed together out on the dance floor, her entire body tingling.

They'd danced, teasing each other with the promise of so much more until she'd reached her breaking point and tugged him outside into the back alley. When she'd framed that bristled jaw in her palms and leaned in to kiss him…

He'd pinned her to the brick wall and reduced her to a panting, mindless mass of need with nothing but that sinful mouth and his hands in her hair.

And then he'd walked away and never called her, because he'd found out who she was. Or rather, that she was Easton's sister.

Charlie wouldn't dare say anything about all that here though. And there had to be something more to this. Some specific reason they would want her for this assignment.

"You know each other and you worked well together during the incident at your family's place," her boss went on. "There's already trust between you, and that's critical for undercover work."

The word *well* might be stretching it a little. Jamie certainly hadn't been too happy with her that night back in September. "There's more. I know there is. So just say it. Why me?" Because there had to be a really specific and big goddamn reason for them to want her for something like this.

Her boss inclined his head, looking a bit guilty. "The things I already said still stand, but yeah, there's more. To put it bluntly, you're Baker's type, exactly. In addition to your skill set, we think you're the best shot we have at gaining access to that laptop."

"What type is that?"

"Brunette. Young. Attractive. Girl next door look."

It felt like a giant fist closed around her stomach and squeezed. "What exactly are you expecting me to do to get access?"

"Nothing physical," he answered immediately. "But once you put yourself out there he's going to make a pass at you, guaranteed. Maybe more than a pass. You need to be ready, and you need to stay close to Rodriguez."

The thought of this Baker guy putting the moves on her made her feel dirty, but she tried not to react outwardly. If her boss thought she could handle this and needed her specifically, then she must have what it took, and he wouldn't ask it of her if it wasn't vital to their investigation.

Though she maintained eye contact with him, she was acutely aware of Jamie seated at the end of the table, arms folded across his wide chest. It drove her nuts because she knew damn well he wasn't always as contained as he'd like people to think. She'd experienced glimpses of the fire that raged beneath that calm surface twice already when he'd let his control slip with her.

Her boss slid a file across the table to her. "For you to peruse later on about Baker. We'll come up with a way to invent an introduction between you two before you meet him in person. From what we know of him, he's a playboy with lots of cash to throw around and he loves to impress the ladies."

Oh, awesome.

"After you meet, it's just a matter of you making the right impression, intriguing him enough to gain access to his house, then getting close enough to that laptop in order to transfer the files. We'll invent a solid cover for you and Rodriguez, and an airtight reason for Baker to want you there.

"After you get the files, you'll never have to see him again, until we nail him and you testify against him in court. But you need to think this over carefully, because while Baker seems like just a rich businessman and we don't believe he's a real physical threat to you, he's got power and connections, not to mention information he wants to hide. There's still a significant level of risk involved in taking this assignment, if he finds out about you or Rodriguez."

Charlie took a deep breath and digested everything he'd said. As an analyst, this was totally out of her scope and job description. It was also a hell of a lot more exciting than her average day sifting through encrypted files on her computer. A challenge. And God knew she could never walk away from one.

She shifted her gaze to her brother, seated next to Hamilton, wanting his input. Or at least his reassurance.

"Whenever you're with Baker, Jamie'll be there to make sure you're safe." Easton's warm brown eyes were solemn, a hint of worry shadowing them. He trusted Jamie with his life on a daily basis, but he didn't know about the attraction between her and his best buddy. Would that have changed his mind? "If you take this on, the agency will make sure you're ready before you start, and then it'll give you adequate protection in case you need a quick extraction at any point during the op."

But Jamie would be the bulk of her protection. "And in the meantime, I've got to get friendly with Baker and lie to his face every time I see him, not to mention stay in character the whole time. I'm not a trained actor." And why the hell wasn't Jamie saying anything? Didn't he have any objections to this? She guessed he would have spoken up long before she'd arrived if he did.

"We need someone with specific technical skills for this job, and your boss told us you're the best in your department," the Fed to her right said. "Not only that, you match Baker's known type perfectly. You're the best fit for this op considering the tight timeframe we're working with, because there will likely be computer expertise required mid-op and we might not be able to establish direct coms with you, depending on how Baker's house and security is set up."

Was he trying to talk her into this, or out of it? "What will my cover be?"

"You'll be known as Spider, a gifted hacker from the dark net. We've been working on a fake ID for her for some time now. That's how we'll make the introduction between you and Baker happen. We've got a team working on introducing a special virus into his business computer system. One of our informants who works with Baker will arrange for the introduction. Based on what we know about Baker, he'll hire you to fix his problem, then, after you gain his trust, we'll go from there."

"Spider," she repeated, feeling number by the minute. This was so surreal.

"You can go by Charlie or Charlotte in person, so it'll be more natural for you. But you'll need a different surname and a background that's close to yours, though different enough to avoid problems later on. You and Rodriguez will pose as neighbors in the same condo building in New York City, so it won't be too far away from Baker's place."

Neighbors? She barely kept her eyes from bugging out. She and Jamie, living side by side as platonic coworkers for an unknown amount of time? After she'd decided to cut him out of her life completely and forget all about him because she refused to allow him to play with her? "Why is Baker so important?"

"He's been laundering money for a good chunk of the *Veneno* cartel. We just haven't been able to prove it yet."

Oh, God. The Venom cartel. One of the most powerful and ruthless narco-organizations the world had ever seen. It was so secret that no one knew who the leader was, only that anyone who crossed him wound up dying a hideous death, along with everyone they cared about. Innocent or guilty, it didn't matter to the *Venenos*.

She steeled herself. "When would the job start?"

"Now," her boss answered bluntly. "After some intensive training to get you ready, you'll both head to NYC in three days' time. The meet with Baker will happen as soon as we can arrange it after that."

Her head was spinning. "How long do I have to think this over?"

"Not long. We need an answer so we can get moving on this, or find someone else." His pale blue eyes delved into hers, his expression earnest. "I want you on this assignment, Charlie. Believe me, the agency and I wouldn't ask this of you if it weren't damned important. The intel on that laptop could be the key in bringing down the entire *Veneno* cartel."

Silence settled over the room, squeezing her from all sides. Everyone was staring at her expectantly. She glanced first at her brother, who was watching her, then at Jamie. That hot caramel gaze met hers unflinchingly and didn't let go.

Studying her. Waiting for an answer. And, if she wasn't mistaken, there was an unspoken challenge there as well.

You game, Trouble?

Yeah, he knew her too well. Agreeing to this whole thing was insane, but she never had been able to resist a dare and the wild streak in her was clamoring for action her desk job just couldn't deliver. And that silent dare from Jamie clinched it.

Mind made up, her heart rate kicked up another notch. Before she could change her mind, she tore her gaze away from that magnetic stare and looked back at her boss. "Okay, I'm in."

An almost proud smile broke over his face. "Okay." Leaning back in his chair, he folded his arms behind his head. "We'll get started on arranging an introduction between Spider and Baker on the dark net."

Chapter Three

Their undercover partnership was off to an ominous start and they hadn't even spoken a single word to each other yet.

As soon as the meeting ended, Jamie jumped out of his seat and hurried out the boardroom door after Charlie. Except for when she'd first entered the room and when her boss had sprung the news about working undercover with him, she hadn't made eye contact with him.

Her unwillingness to even look at him was driving him crazy, almost an invisible itch skittering across his skin.

One, because he'd already tasted that luscious mouth and felt that lean body pressed to his. He'd thought about her nonstop these past seven months, kept tabs on her through Easton while trying not to seem overly interested in his best buddy's sister. And two, because she and him were going to be working together closely over the coming weeks.

Real closely. And while they did, they had to set personal differences/friction—such as the intense attraction between them and their differing opinions on what to do about it—aside until the job was done.

Due to his position at the far end of the table, he was the last one out the door. Charlie was a few people ahead of him, talking to Easton as they headed for the elevator at the other end of the hall, and stepped inside before he could reach her.

Their eyes met briefly as he entered the crowded space, but she looked away quickly and stared straight ahead as the doors slid shut. He stifled a sigh and tamped down his annoyance. They were going to have to clear the air between them, fast.

At the first floor, everyone filed out into the lobby and Charlie immediately swept right past him without a word, spine ramrod straight, head held high. Cool and distant, the total opposite of the woman who'd all but melted in his arms that night at her family's place.

Yeah, not going to work, pequeña.

He exchanged a loaded look with Easton, then went after her. "Charlie," he called out before she reached the exit.

She stopped at the tinted glass front doors, facing away from him, long, coffee-brown hair spilling in a shiny waterfall down the middle of her rigid back. When he caught up to her she glanced over and met his gaze, her expression guarded.

"I need to talk to you," he said, keeping his voice low.

She stared up at him with espresso-colored eyes for a long moment, then relented, her normally lush mouth compressed into a thin line. "All right, fine. For a minute." She turned around and took a step toward the couches set in the center of the lobby.

Nuh-uh. They weren't talking here where someone might overhear them and a half-dozen security cameras would pick up their every move.

He caught her elbow. "No. Somewhere with a little more privacy." She huffed out an irritated breath but didn't resist as he tugged her toward the doors.

Cool spring evening air rushed over them when they stepped outside, the chilly wind and ominous gray clouds promising rain and giving him the perfect excuse to usher her across the lit parking lot to his truck. He opened the passenger door for her, waited for her to get in, then rounded the hood and slid into the driver's seat.

Her sweet scent seemed to swirl around the enclosed space, taunting him. She sat facing him at an angle against the plush leather seat, arms folded across her chest and her expression closed. "So? What do you want to talk about?"

So many things, most of which he couldn't say. Wouldn't. So that left only one safe option. "The op."

She lifted a dark eyebrow, cocked her head slightly. "You sure? You wouldn't rather talk about why you kissed me like that on my father's back lawn after I'd just shot a man to death, then tried to sneak out without saying goodbye and dropped off the radar again for the past seven months?"

He withheld a sigh. Even though he should have expected it by now, her directness still took him off guard. So fine. He'd say it. "You know why." He'd told her point blank that night in September.

I play for keeps.

The words hovered in the air between them. A warning and a promise. There was no way she'd forgotten or could have misinterpreted what he'd meant. And he still meant it now. He refused to be a one-night stand for her, and would never indulge in a casual fling with a teammate's sister, let alone his best friend's.

"You're serious? That's it?" she asked, sounding incredulous as the other eyebrow rose to join the first. "It's been seven months without a word from you, even when I reached out to you through Easton. After everything that happened that night, I expected more from you."

His jaw tensed. "I know exactly how long it's been. And I sent a message back through your brother." Something benign and totally innocent, but enough to be polite without giving away his feelings for her. If she knew how into her he really was, she'd use it and try to play him to get what she wanted. Them, in bed together. And then she'd move on soon after.

No way would he let it happen.

Charlie let out a humorless laugh. "Wow. Okay then."

She had no damn idea how hard it had been not to contact her. He'd kept his distance from her this entire time because he was way too aware of the fine line he was walking with her, and because she tested his control in a way no other woman ever had. The truth was, in addition to wanting her, he *liked* her.

A lot.

He admired the hell out of her smarts, her courage and the skill she'd shown that night in the forest, even if he'd been pissed that she'd run out ahead of him like that. It had shaken him because he hadn't been able to protect her and she could have gotten seriously hurt or killed if she hadn't fired first—and hit what she'd been aiming at. "Yeah, I'm dead serious."

She studied his eyes a long moment, as though trying to figure out if he was bullshitting her or not. "What, so you're waiting for me to make the next move?" she said on a laugh, as if she still couldn't quite believe it.

"Only if you're all in. Otherwise I'm not interested."

"All in," she murmured, looking equal parts fascinated and baffled. As if no man had ever passed up the chance of a fling with her. And maybe they hadn't. But Jamie wasn't like the other guys she'd been with, and

33

he wanted her to know it.

"That's right. It's just the way I'm wired." The hell of it was, he knew damn well she wasn't ready for him. At least not for the intensity of what he wanted from her. She was Easton's sister for Christ's sake, he wasn't going to simply screw around with her and then walk away.

Except she'd made it clear she wasn't interested in anything serious or long term. So why was she so pissed at him then? She wanted to play, to try him on for size just to see what the fit was like. A temporary thrill before she moved on to the next conquest. No strings, no commitments. Just fun and pleasure.

She was used to guys looking to have a good time and then just walk away. Most guys would jump at the chance for a hookup with her, but he was so far beyond all that bullshit with Charlie. He couldn't do short and casual with her even if he'd wanted to. He wasn't a toy to be used.

He was thirty-one years old and done with playing. He knew what he wanted from her, and it wasn't a one-night stand.

So no. If she wanted him, it was going to be all or nothing.

"So. The op," he said, changing the subject and bringing them back to the most pressing issue at hand. In all honesty, part of him still couldn't believe this was actually happening. Right up until she'd agreed to be part of the op he'd expected her to bow out, and now that she'd committed, they had no choice but to see this thing through. "You've got a file on Baker now, but let me save you some reading time and sum it up for you in one line." He paused a beat. "He's a human piece of shit."

She gave a slow nod, searching his eyes, all business now. "Define 'shit'."

Where to start? "He's worth at least eighty million, easy. On the surface, he projects the image he wants everyone to see, a big time real estate developer on the east coast. Intel from the flash drive you helped crack the encryption on says otherwise, pointing to various offshore companies he might be involved with.

"According to Gallant, originally the guy made his fortune arranging cocaine shipments coming into the States from the Gulf, and when that got too hot, he switched to laundering money for himself and his cartel buddies. Most of the assets he owns are paid for with laundered money, and Gallant says once the agency digs deeper, it'll find more."

"Well they must not have much on him, if they were desperate enough to bring me in to an undercover op to steal the files from his personal laptop."

"They don't have *enough*," he corrected. He needed her to know exactly what she was getting into. If she wanted to change her mind, it wasn't too late. And truth be told, he'd rather she said no. Watching her risk her life once was enough for him. He wasn't eager to see her do it a second time, even if she was the most technically qualified person who matched Baker's "type".

"To get enough evidence to nail him with and then put him away, they need a lot more than what they have," he continued. "And make no mistake, he's still dangerous, with an unknown number of kills under his belt. If the agency's right, he's one of a long list of people working for *el Escorpion*." The most wanted narco-terrorist in the Western hemisphere.

Recognition flared in her dark eyes.

Okay, she knew the name, realized what it meant. Good. That meant she'd understand the stakes. "Yeah, so you know what kind of person Baker is underneath that slick businessman image he hides behind. He's a notorious playboy, so you'll have to watch out for that." He didn't worry about that part as much as the rest of it. Charlie was a force to be reckoned with. "Aside from

35

however many kills he's personally responsible for by his own hand, Baker is suspected of having ordered the murders of at least a half-dozen people that we know about, and there are likely more. So this is still going to be risky, even though I know you can defend yourself if need be. We both need to be prepared."

"I know."

She still seemed determined to go through with it. "We're going to keep your contact with him to a minimum and a backup team will always be nearby, just in case. My job is to make sure you're safe, plain and simple. But there might be times when I can't be in the room with you and Baker, and we'll just have to work around that."

"I understand."

She didn't appear apprehensive at all, no surprise. She'd never let on that she was nervous. He didn't want to scare her, but he needed her to be on guard. "If we do this, then you're going to have to follow my lead and do exactly what I say. If I give you an order, you follow it, no questions asked. Or this isn't going to work."

A spark of resentment lit her eyes at his heavy-handedness, but he didn't care. None of what had happened between them before mattered a damn now. From this point on, they were a team. She'd never done anything like this before and her safety came first. He'd do whatever it took to keep her focused and safe, even if it meant alienating her later.

"Fine. Anything else?"

Some of the tension in his gut eased. But yeah, there was one more thing he needed to know. "Do you trust me?" It was critical to him that she did. If she didn't, he'd walk away from this whole assignment and have his boss replace him with someone else from the team. No matter how much he'd hate placing Charlie's well-being in a teammate's hands.

"Yes," she answered, no hesitation.

Her response made him breathe easier. "Good." She was his responsibility and he didn't take that lightly. No matter what, he'd make sure she came out of this unharmed. He'd sworn it to Easton and now he'd vow it to her. "I'll keep you safe. I promise."

Something flickered in her eyes. A softness. Then it was gone and she was all focused energy again. "Okay."

That brief glimmer of softness did things to him.

Charlie had an edge to her, and it was sharp enough to cut when she wanted it to. But he'd seen the sweetness in her too, along with the heat, and that rare show of vulnerability after she'd killed that shooter in the woods.

It had twisted him into knots to let her go that night, to walk away. She had no clue how badly he'd wanted to scoop her up right there at the farmhouse's front door and take her to a hotel where they could be alone together, then strip off her clothes and comfort her with his body in the most elemental way there was.

All night long, until she trusted him on the deepest level possible and realized he was the one for her.

That's ultimately why he'd left. He'd never felt this protective or territorial of any woman, and it jarred him.

"Good," he answered.

Silence spread between them and he didn't try to fill it. This job could take weeks. Maybe even longer, if Baker was suspicious. Did he have the strength to ignore the pull he felt toward her, when she stirred his deepest desires in a way no one else ever had?

Charlie lowered her arms and straightened in her seat, shifting her gaze to look out the windshield. "It's a job, Jamie. Few weeks max, hopefully less. We're both professionals. We'll just have to make the best of it." Without pause she gathered her purse and reached for the door handle. "See you tomorrow, bright and early so we can get started on our cover assignments."

He didn't stop her. Just sat there and let her go. It wouldn't do him any good to call her back, and he'd said the most important things anyhow.

Releasing a sigh, he watched her walk across the well-lit lot to her car, that shapely ass swaying in those snug jeans, and struggled to rein in his thoughts.

Thoughts of her naked, under him. Bent over in front of him. On her back, tied to his bed, eyes glassy with lust, cheeks flushed, bare breasts heaving with each ragged breath she took while he showed her one more reason why he was worth going all in for.

So many times over the past seven months he'd imagined what sounds she'd make as he pleasured her, teased her until she was ready to beg. So many times he'd stroked himself off thinking of the look on her face at the moment she surrendered to him.

Shaking off the thoughts, he drew a deep breath, his gaze still following her over to her car. He waited until she slipped inside and drove away before starting the ignition. As he pulled out of the parking lot and headed home to his empty condo, he couldn't shake the lingering unease settling in his chest.

If anything happened to her on his watch, he'd never forgive himself.

Chapter Four

❖◇❖◇❖

"Thanks so much for lunch, Mr. Baker. I'll speak with my lawyer and consider your offer carefully."

Dean tamped down his impatience and pasted on a smile for his female lunch companion, seated across the table from him in the swanky Manhattan café he'd invited her to for this meeting. She wasn't a businesswoman. Was way out of her depth with someone of his caliber.

Unlike her, he'd had to work for everything he had.

Ten years ago the newly rich little heiress might have been hot, with the right makeup and some implants to fill out the top of that designer dress. Now in her early forties, the signs of age were stamped all over her face. The crow's feet and faint wrinkles forming in her cheeks ruined her looks completely.

"You do that," he murmured, already planning his next move. He'd made a fair offer for the lakefront property. He wanted it bad. It was prime real estate, and with the project he had in mind, he could easily give his clients a safe place to invest their money where the feds would never find it.

When her miserly father had died and left her all his assets several months ago, including a parcel of undeveloped land worth fifty million easy, she'd gone from lower middle class, single mother of two, to filthy rich overnight.

Now she had nannies to drive her kids around, a maid to clean her new mansion and a personal chef to do the cooking. It was no secret she liked the high life she could now afford, dressing in designer label clothes and driving a brand new Tesla instead of the second-hand Ford she'd driven for the last eight years.

Dean knew, because he'd checked. He knew everything about her. He made a point of knowing everything about a target before ever establishing contact, in case he needed to use it later.

The woman set her napkin down and made to push her chair back, so Dean stood and quickly rounded the table to pull it out for her. She flashed him a startled smile, her cheeks flushing pink.

Yeah, she liked the show of manners and wasn't used to male attention. The ex she'd been married to for almost twenty years obviously had given up on romancing her long ago. Maybe if she'd put a little more effort into maintaining her looks and body, he would have tried harder.

"Thank you," she murmured, gathering her purse before standing, the gigantic diamond ring on her finger catching in the light. She wore it on her right hand, no doubt so people would see it every time she reached for her water glass or scratched the end of her nose.

Dean could smell her lack of self-esteem a mile away. She could wrap herself in expensive clothes and jewels and live in a ten-million-dollar mansion in Connecticut, but it would never fill the emptiness inside her. No, that kind of confidence could only come from inside a person, and she just didn't have it.

She glanced up at him through her false lashes, her look bordering on flirtatious. "I'll let you know by the weekend."

"Okay." She wasn't going to accept the deal, he could already tell, and that annoyed the hell out of him. He'd have to make another, higher offer. If she didn't accept that one...

Well, there were always other methods he could employ to get the answer he wanted if she proved difficult. He hadn't needed to resort to them recently. Whenever possible he preferred not resorting to violence. It made his life a lot easier when things didn't get messy.

For now, he'd wait. Give her a day or two to think about his offer, then push. He'd learned over the years that people reacted more favorably to pressure after a short waiting period, rather than right away. Just one of the things he'd figured out during the process of making the transition from a thug to a civilized businessman.

But still ruthless, even if people didn't see it until it was too late.

He caught her hand, noted the flash of surprise in her eyes, the wariness, as he slowly raised it to his mouth and pressed his lips to the back of it, just above the gaudy ring. Her cheeks flushed darker, and that shy little smile was downright endearing, even with the wrinkles. She saw only the veneer he showed to the rest of the world, the polished, successful real estate developer with the suave manners.

He took a certain perverse pleasure in knowing she had no idea who she was really dealing with.

"Pleasure to meet you face-to-face finally, Catherine," he murmured against her soft skin.

"Y-yes. Nice to meet you too." Still blushing, she pulled her hand away, nervously smoothed it down the front of her dress.

She was sweet in a way, almost innocent. It intrigued him, made him wonder how she would respond if he drugged her and did the kinds of things to her that her ex probably hadn't dreamed of.

Maybe he'd do it after they closed the deal. Take her out to his place in the Hamptons and fuck her for the night. He'd slip something into her drink when she wasn't looking, some of the new product that was going around. A small dose would leave her conscious but not aware, and he could do any damn thing he liked to her. When it was over and she woke up alone in a hotel room the next morning, he'd have the land and she wouldn't remember a thing.

He'd done it before, though the women he'd chosen weren't linked to him through business, and usually younger and hotter. Still, he could make an exception for her this once. She wasn't hideous, and the thought of defiling her that way sent a wave of power through his veins, settling in his groin with a pleasurable ache. It had been too long since he'd let his inner deviant out to play.

He shifted to block the sight of his swelling erection in case she happened to glance down and gestured to the door with another easy smile. "Shall we?" He set a hand on her lower back, keeping the contact light, non-threatening, but a shade possessive. She didn't protest or pull away, shooting him another glance from under her lashes.

Outside the restaurant, a cool breeze tugged at his suit jacket. In between the skyscrapers of the concrete jungle that was downtown Manhattan, slices of pure blue sky were visible. A gorgeous spring day.

He hailed a cab for her, even opened the back door and paid the fare before he put her in the backseat. She shot him one last smile and waved as the cab pulled away from the curb. He was still hard, arousal swirling through him at the thought of what he could do to her.

Feeling energized, he turned and headed south up the sidewalk, pulling out his phone to call his secretary back at the office. It was only a ten-minute walk and the weather was perfect for it. "Did they fix the issue yet?"

"No," she answered. "They've tried everything."

Annoyance burst inside him. This was the third tech company this week that hadn't been able to figure out why his supposedly "secure" and insanely expensive state-of-the-art computer system at Pinnacle Group was continually being infected by a complex and vicious virus.

Whoever was behind it had fucked up the whole system and so far no one had been able to figure out a solution. "Tell them to forget it, and that I'll only pay them half their fee. Then get on the phone and find someone who can fix the system."

"Yes, sir."

He ended the call without responding and headed for the curb to hail a cab. It pissed him off so much that someone was fucking with his system.

Unacceptable. He'd been expecting an important wire transfer the other day and because of certain…delicate alterations he had to make before it went into his bank account, he had to run it through his specialized system at the office.

Except the virus made that impossible. If he didn't get the issue resolved in the next day or two, certain high-profile clients would demand answers. Attention he didn't want and couldn't afford.

Dammit, he might have to make the two-hour drive to his place in Sagaponack and run the transfer through his encrypted laptop. But that was risky because if anyone at the bank or a government agency traced it, they might launch an investigation. He'd only do it as a last resort.

This business was fluid, and considering the kind of people he dealt with, he was only as good as his reputation. And his rep was only as good as his last job or transaction. He was an important man and had important people to keep happy if he wanted his lifestyle and position within the cartel to last.

An available taxi came into view as traffic began flowing toward him again. He started to lift his hand, then an idea occurred to him and he lowered it, turning away to head back into the tide of people moving along the sidewalk. He reached into his inside breast coat pocket and took out the special, encrypted phone he only used for his private business ventures.

"I was just going to call you," Tim, his most trusted source said. "The meeting in Tampa is a go."

Three of the big bosses and their enforcers were holding a summit at a hotel Dean's company owned on the waterfront. "That's good news." Best he'd heard all day. "You got them the penthouse apartments?"

"Of course."

"Good. See to the usual arrangements for our guests."

"Already done."

Dean had long ago become a master of being able to do dirty business in public without tipping anyone off. To anyone near enough to hear him—or anyone listening in on the off chance that someone had managed to tap his phone without his knowledge—the conversation would sound totally benign.

The only way to stay out of prison was not to get caught in the first place, and he made sure he paid his people well enough to buy their loyalty—and their silence. "Keep me informed. But that's not what I called about."

"Okay, what's up?"

"I need a computer expert to fix an ongoing problem I'm having with a virus in my office building's computer system. I haven't alerted local authorities about the attack, for obvious reasons. You've got your trusted contacts for that kind of thing." Almost all of whom were deeply entrenched in the criminal underworld. "Know of anyone who could help?"

"You want someone legit?"

"I want someone who can take care of this within the next twenty-four hours."

Tim didn't answer for a moment. "There's been a lot of chatter recently about someone I've heard of through a trusted source. Operates strictly on the dark net."

"Go on."

"Some hacker wizard, goes by the name Spider."

"Can you contact him, make an offer and tell him I'll make it worth his while? I want this dealt with in the next day or two. I'm tired of dealing with this shit. I have business to take care of and I don't trust anyone else to find someone."

"I'll see what I can do."

Two stoplights ahead, the cab Catherine rode in turned right at the corner, passing another building his company owned, and had built from the ground up. Dean smiled to himself.

If she knew the measures he'd taken to secure such a prime location—or what was hidden beneath the building itself—Catherine would have been too afraid to turn down the offer he'd made today.

****

This was more frustrating than she'd bargained for, and it was supposed to be the simplest part of the entire operation.

Charlie made a sound of irritation in the back of her throat and adjusted the magnifying glasses on the end of her nose while she fiddled with the chip held between the pincers of the tweezers. Spring sunshine streamed through the window of the fourth-floor Brooklyn apartment building she'd moved into three days ago...

Along with her sexy neighbor currently occupying apartment 4D.

It still felt surreal that she was doing this—about to go on an undercover op, let alone with Jamie. The past few days had gone by in a blur of activity, a string of long-ass days full of meetings and briefings as the agency rushed to prep her for her upcoming role as Spider. Hard as it was to ignore her attraction to him and the growing feelings she'd thus far unsuccessfully tried to bury, she couldn't deny that she felt better knowing he was right next door.

They'd gone over their individual cover stories together until she could repeat them in her sleep, and she'd memorized everything in the file on Baker as well in addition to all the other information the agency insisted she master before coming to New York. She was now Charlotte Cooper, website designer by day and revered dark net hacker Spider by night.

A knock at the door signaled her guest was here for the meeting.

Charlie rose from the kitchen table, excited to meet the real Spider, who the DEA had brought in to be part of this op. The agency wanted the two of them to meet in person so Charlie could ask questions and add certain details to help her cover story be even more solid.

She checked the peephole before answering, then opened the door, barely covering her surprise as she stared at the woman. "Liz?"

"Yes, nice to meet you." The fifty-something, heavy-set DEA contractor wore a green sweater set and a gray wool skirt. Her salt-and-pepper hair was styled into a tidy chin-length bob and the strand of pearls around her neck matched the ones in her ears.

She looked like Mrs. Claus. Or at least someone's grandma.

The woman known as Spider shook Charlie's hand and marched inside with her bag over her shoulder, the lenses of her black cat-eye glasses catching the light streaming in through the kitchen windows. "You ready to do this?"

Charlie shut the door and ushered her toward the kitchen table. "Yes. You've got perfect timing. Maybe you can figure out how to make this damn thing work." She gestured to the chip and the plastic lip-gloss tube.

She had a team to help her work on it, but she'd wanted to do it herself. If she was going to use it on the op, she needed to know exactly how it all fit together. No one knew for sure what kind of security measures Baker had at his office or vacation home, so she'd made sure to use minimal metallic parts in case there was some kind of metal detector.

"Ooh, I like it." Liz picked up the tube, examined it for a long moment, then gestured for the tweezers.

Charlie handed them over without a word and watched in amazement as Liz expertly slipped the chip into the base of the tube, then secured it with a wadded-up elastic band tamped beneath it into the base.

"Hand me the top so I can see if this will pass inspection." Liz took the lid and snapped it into place, then took the lid off and twisted the stick of lip-gloss up and out of the tube. With a satisfied grunt, she handed it back to Charlie.

Charlie turned it over in her fingers, looking for a seam, any sign at all that the plastic had been tampered with. "Wow, you're good. A little scary how fast you figured that out, considering I've been sitting here farting around with it for twenty minutes."

"I've just got more years of experience on you, that's all. So, Charlie." She leaned back in her chair, plump hands folded neatly over her rounded belly. "Got any tea and munchies around here? I'm starving."

After serving her guest, Charlie sat down and got better acquainted with Spider.

"I'm guessing nobody showed you a picture of me before I showed up, huh?" Liz asked before taking a sip of tea, her bright blue eyes sparkling with humor from within the frames of her glasses.

The agency had scrambled to put a file together on Spider for Charlie, but given the rush it hadn't contained a photo, just mostly technical stuff about her online activity, and Liz had just flown into NYC last night. "No. It's just that you're one of the best hackers out there, and that your day job is in the IT field."

Liz snorted. "I'm an elementary school librarian from Wisconsin and I'm about to become a grandma for the third time."

Charlie's eyes widened and she couldn't help a smile. "Really?" That hadn't been in the file either.

"Yep on both counts. Going on seventeen years at the school. I love my job."

"And how did you get involved in your…" Not a hobby. Calling the kind of hacking Liz did a hobby was downright insulting. "Extracurricular activities?"

Liz's lips curved upward in a sly smile. "My ex-husband was a NYC detective. I knew he was cheating on me, and didn't trust any locals to help me get evidence. So I used my IT background, took up delving into the dark net as a hobby, and everything went from there."

Wow. "Did you catch him?"

"Oh yeah. Divorced his cheating ass and got a nice settlement he's still paying for through spousal support."

Charlie laughed. She loved this woman. "Good for you."

Liz grinned. "Yep. And then the woman he'd been cheating on me with wound up giving him gonorrhea."

Laughing, she put her mug down on the table. "So, let's get down to business, shall we?"

The DEA had already briefed Liz on the investigation and upcoming operation, since she was an official informant for the agency. "Yes."

An hour later, Charlie was even more impressed with the woman sitting across from her. No, more like awed and astounded. The woman wore frumpy sweater sets and pearls and looked like the most harmless woman in the entire world. But she was actually a predator in her own right, using her skills to unleash havoc on criminals she later exposed.

"Anything else?" Liz asked when she finished detailing how Charlie was to "fix" Baker's computer system, then helped herself to another cup of tea.

Charlie's mind was spinning. "One thing."

"Shoot."

"Why stop now? I mean, now that the agency is using you as an informant and given me part of your identity to use as a cover, your anonymity is over."

Liz shrugged a shoulder. "It was time. I love the idea of going out with a bang, using my skills to help bring down a cartel." Her eyes glittered with excitement. "I'm ready to pack it in and spend more time with my grandbabies before they're too old to want to hang out with me."

"When this is all over, promise me we'll meet up again so you can tell me more about the virus you designed for Baker's computer system."

Another evil smile. "Some of my best work. What I wouldn't have given to be a fly on the wall when your team uploaded it into his system."

At the brisk knock on the door, Charlie's stomach buzzed with that increasingly familiar combination of nerves and butterflies. "That'll be my new neighbor."

"Mmm, and it must be such a hardship, living next

to a man like that," Liz said with a conspiratorial wink. She'd met Jamie earlier at a meeting Charlie hadn't attended because she'd been busy with the people from her department.

Charlie didn't answer as she went over to open the door, steeling herself for the sight that awaited her.

Jamie stood there looking all rugged and sexy. Even though she'd prepared herself, he still made her heart beat faster. The fiercely independent part of her still rankled at the idea of him expecting her to capitulate to his terms if she wanted to pursue things between them. Given their current situation, she couldn't avoid him. Ignoring the attraction wasn't working, but she sure as hell wasn't going to agree to his ridiculous terms either.

I play for keeps. Really? Well, he didn't get to call the shots on that. No man dictated to her how she ran her life.

"Hey," she murmured, stepping back to let him in. She'd done her best to overlook her attraction to him, but it was impossible to do it convincingly when he was living literally next door. Every time she heard the old building's pipes groan in the wall between their apartments she imagined him standing naked under the shower spray, water sluicing down that hard male body.

His dark-honey gaze warmed as he smiled a little, softening the rugged masculinity of his face. "Hey." He walked in, his big frame making the cozy space feel so much smaller with his restless, commanding energy. "Good meeting?" he asked, nodding at Liz.

"Great," Charlie answered. "Just hope I can do the real Spider justice."

"Honey, trust me, I'm already flattered. The real Spider never looked so sexy, even back when I was in my twenties." She tipped her head slightly, gave Jamie an appreciative look before winking at Charlie.

If he noticed, Jamie didn't let on. He turned to face

Charlie, hands on hips, the afternoon sunlight gilding his broad shoulders and highlighting the sculpted muscles in his arms and chest under his T-shirt. It wasn't fair that he was being so damn stubborn about them, even if she wouldn't start something while they were on this job together.

Did he ever think about her? Fantasize about her when he lay alone in bed, or in the shower, with only mere inches of plaster and drywall separating them? She wanted him to be suffering too.

"Just got word from the team," he said to her. "Baker took the bait. Our informant contacted Spider on his behalf. He's called you in."

Charlie's pulse sped up and she looked over at Liz. "What's your usual procedure for contacting someone in a situation like this?"

Liz shrugged. "Burner phone while I'm out doing errands. I've never made an in-person service call of course, usually I either work remotely or walk a client through it over the phone." She raised her tea mug in salute. "You'll do great."

Hope so. A lot's riding on this. She nodded at Jamie. "I'll go get a phone." The agency had given them several disposable, encrypted phones so that their calls couldn't be traced back to them.

She alerted the team that she was about to make a call, then slowed her breathing as she dialed the number she'd been given. Probably not Baker. Someone who worked for him, maybe. The team would be trying to trace the guy's phone, but likely wouldn't be able to find him if he was using an encrypted phone.

"I heard you were looking for me?" she asked when the man answered.

"Spider?"

"Depends."

"I'm calling on behalf of a prospective client," he

said.

"Why didn't he or she contact me personally?"

A derisive sound. "You're not the only one who wants to protect their identity."

She paused, making sure to proceed with the caution appropriate for someone with Spider's reputation. "I'm listening. What's the problem?"

He told her about the virus, and that no one could figure out how to fix it. "So my client's hoping you can help. His office is right here in Manhattan. You interested?"

"Maybe. But I don't usually make house calls. It'll cost you." She glanced at Jamie, who was over at the table with Liz, both of them watching her with their chins propped in one hand.

"I understand. My client's prepared to make it worth your while."

"How much?"

"Ten thousand for coming out to look at it. Another twenty if you can fix it."

Thirty k for getting rid of a virus. Baker really was desperate. "Oh, I can fix it." The real Spider had just told her exactly how to. "If I agree to do this, your client needs to understand that my identity must be kept a secret. Because if he tries to expose me, he'll regret it."

"Of course. Believe me, we have as much interest in exposing you as we do of being exposed ourselves."

Because they were afraid she'd be able to hack into Baker's computer and find something to incriminate him with, then go public with it before they could stop her.

"Good." She paused another moment, letting him think she was mulling over his offer, when in fact it was already a foregone conclusion. "Okay, I'll do it. Tomorrow morning, six o'clock. Before anyone else arrives. I'll need the address."

Jamie was still watching her when she ended the call

a moment later. "Well?" he asked, leaning back in the chair, that magnetic amber gaze making her lower belly flip.

"The op's a go. Tomorrow at oh-six-hundred."

Liz smiled as she raised the rim of her cup to her lips. "And the Spider will catch herself another fly."

Chapter Five

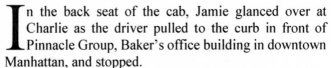

In the back seat of the cab, Jamie glanced over at Charlie as the driver pulled to the curb in front of Pinnacle Group, Baker's office building in downtown Manhattan, and stopped.

Charlie sat perfectly still beside him, staring straight out her window, had barely said a word to him since leaving Brooklyn. She wasn't annoyed with him as far as he knew, so he guessed she must be mentally preparing.

"You want to go over anything again?" he asked after he paid the driver and they climbed out onto the curb.

"No, I'm good." She tugged at the hem of her short black leather jacket that stopped just below her waist, and straightened her shoulders.

The slim-fitting dark jeans she wore hugged every curve of her hips and ass, and her legs looked even longer with the high-heeled leather boots. She wore her dark hair loose around her shoulders, some smoky eye makeup and bright red lipstick. When she stepped into his office, Baker was going to love what he saw.

An unexpected twinge of jealousy stabbed Jamie and

he pushed it aside.

He glanced up at the tall glass-fronted building before them, then back at her. This was her first time doing anything like this, so she had to be nervous, even if she was hiding it well. He was nervous for her too. "You'll do great, and I'll be right there with you."

Those dark eyes shifted to him, so serious, but her expression softened a little as her lips curved upward. "I'll do my best. Ready?"

"Take your time." He resisted the impulse to take her hand or smooth a hand over her hair, needing to soothe her nerves. "We won't go in until you're ready."

"I'm ready," she said. "Waiting will just make me more nervous."

"Okay." They'd prepared for this as best they could, and the rest of the team was waiting in a van a couple blocks away, ready for Charlie to transmit a few files from Baker's office computer system.

The real Spider could have hacked it, but the whole purpose of this "test" op was for Charlie to establish a rapport and some trust with Baker, and to check the transmitter on his office computer system. They needed to know what modifications needed to be made with the device for if and when he and Charlie got an invite to Baker's house so she could try to access his private laptop there.

Neither of them could risk wearing a wire for this op. If Baker was suspicious enough to search them and found one, the whole op would be blown and they might be in danger. Should anything go wrong, Jamie was to get Charlie out of the building and clear of danger, then meet up with the backup team at a pre-chosen location.

He gestured forward with one hand. "After you."

She strode for the front doors, her gait and posture radiating a confidence that bordered on cocky.

Jamie followed a few steps behind her. Given his line

of work and his level of training, it was intuitive to keep his head on a swivel at a time like this, watching for threats. It was hard to keep from looking around, but his cover was as a personal trainer, so he had to tone it down, along with his protectiveness toward Charlie. He was here as her neighbor, nothing more, and had to act the part.

Inside the lobby a two-man security team was waiting for them. "Who's this?" one of them asked her, nodding at Jamie.

"My neighbor. I asked him to come here with me."

Jamie stuck his hands in the kangaroo pouch of his hoodie and didn't say anything as he subtly took note of their surroundings. The expansive lobby was all glass and granite, high-end and sparkling clean. The air held a faint scent of bleach. They appeared to be the only people in here, not surprising given that it was so early yet.

As he gazed around he spotted several security cameras tucked up into the corners of the room near the high ceilings. After making a mental note of their location, he focused on the guards again.

The two men exchanged a glance before looking back at Charlie. "You're to go up alone."

"I won't go up there without him." Her voice was firm, calm, not a trace of nerves.

The taller man's lips compressed in annoyance, then he walked behind the front desk to pick up a telephone. Jamie couldn't hear what he said, but the man was obviously informing Baker of his presence.

Less than a minute later the guard hung up and approached them again. "All right, he can go up too. But not until we check you both for weapons. Standard procedure."

"Of course," Charlie answered, then turned to Jamie. "Sorry about this."

"No problem," he murmured, trying to look as non-threatening as possible as the men approached.

The men took away their phones—specially encrypted by Charlie and her team for this op in case Baker's people tried to access what was on them—checked them for weapons, and even put them through a metal detector. They passed the first major hurdle when the lip-gloss case hiding the transmitter went undetected.

"Mr. Baker's already up in his office waiting for you," the shorter guard said, and escorted them to the elevator. He rode with them to the top floor but didn't get out. It made Jamie edgy to be up here unarmed, but there was no help for it.

A stylishly-dressed woman in her mid-thirties was there to greet them. "I'm Mr. Baker's personal assistant," she said with a smile. "Can I get either of you some coffee or tea?"

"No, thank you," Charlie answered.

"Okay then, right this way." She headed down the carpeted hall and stopped at the door at the end. "The computer expert is here, sir."

The door opened a moment later. Baker stood there in a charcoal business suit and red power tie, his dark blond hair neatly swept to one side.

His brown gaze settled on Charlie and swept over the length of her body once before switching to Jamie with a frown. "Why did you bring your neighbor here? That wasn't part of our arrangement."

Charlie shrugged a shoulder. "This is out of the ordinary for me. I'm only here because my contact convinced me to take the job. Never met you before, so being a single female, I wasn't coming alone."

One side of Baker's mouth pulled up as he watched her. "Smart girl." He looked her over a second time before shifting his attention to Jamie. "And what is it you do, James?"

"I'm a personal trainer." *Who will knock you unconscious without a second's hesitation if you touch her the wrong way.*

"He's not thrilled about being here, because I made him miss a standing appointment with a regular client of his to come with me," Charlie said. "So can we get going on this?"

Baker's gaze flashed to her, a hint of censure there at her bossiness. But so far she was playing her part to perfection. Confident. Direct. No-nonsense. "Am I supposed to call you Spider?"

"Charlie's fine."

He nodded once, not moving a muscle as he stared at her. Silently sizing her up. To her credit, Charlie didn't flinch. "All right then, Charlie. But just you in my office. He stays out here."

"Fine, as long as you leave the door open."

Baker gave another half-smile that made Jamie's skin crawl. "So cautious," he murmured, and set a proprietary hand on Charlie's lower back, just above her ass where the leather jacket stopped.

Jamie hated the way the asshole looked at her. Like he was both fascinated and already imagining getting her naked. "Right this way."

Charlie shot the man a warning look and pulled out of his reach, then walked into the huge office that overlooked the East River. Baker's low chuckle trailed out the door as he followed.

Jamie lowered himself onto an upholstered bench in the hallway and positioned himself so he could see into the office. With the door open he had good sight lines on Charlie, now seated at Baker's desk. The man stood behind her, not even trying to be subtle about looking down the front of her top as he looked over her shoulder.

It put Jamie's teeth on edge. He knew Baker's type, knew how they thought and what lengths some of them would go to in order to get a woman to sleep with them. Or worse, if the woman they wanted wasn't willing.

Charlie must have been irritated by the crowding too, because she turned her head and aimed a hard look at Baker. "Do you mind giving me some space? I'm trying to work here."

The man seemed almost amused by her directness as he eased back a step or two.

Jamie took a slow, deep breath and rested his head back against the wall, trying to appear bored when he was anything but. Shutting off the possessiveness he felt for Charlie was way harder than he'd imagined.

To take his mind off the way Baker was ogling her, he took the opportunity to glance around. All the other offices up here had their doors shut and as far as he could tell they were empty. The only exits were the elevator and the stairwell next to it.

Charlie knew what to do if they needed to get out. If the op went to hell for some reason, she was to leave the building any way she could—even if it meant leaving him behind to deal with the threat—then meet at the emergency extraction point where the backup team would take over.

She had the device with her to test it, but only if she felt safe enough. They didn't want to risk tipping their hand by arousing Baker's suspicion, and they still didn't know how or if they'd get an invite to his place in The Hamptons.

Jamie scanned the far end of the hallway, noting the different kinds of art hanging on the walls. And one object in particular that would allow them the perfect segue into deepening Charlie's connection with Baker.

It was perfect.

"Hey, Charlie, get a load of this."

She glanced over at him from the desk with an annoyed frown. "I'm busy. Can't it wait?"

"Yeah, I guess."

Sighing, she glanced over her shoulder at Baker.

"Sorry, one second." Then she focused back on Jamie. "What?"

"There's a gun in the hall."

A tiny crease appeared on her forehead, but he caught the leap of understanding in her eyes. "What kind of gun?"

"I dunno." He knew exactly what it was. "Bet you'll like it."

"Are you a collector?" Baker asked her with new interest, and straightened.

"Not personally." She pushed the plush office chair back from the desk and strode out into the hallway. "Where?" she asked Jamie, glancing around.

He pointed to the antique rifle mounted in a display case near the far end of the hall.

"Oh, an Enfield!" She hurried over to gaze up at it, then looked back at Baker, who'd followed her. "Is it yours?"

He blinked at her. "Yes."

She studied it a moment longer. "It's in great condition. What year is it?"

"1863."

"Is it Union or Confederate?"

He seemed both surprised and impressed that she'd asked. "Confederate, but it's a non-issue. Was never actually used in the war." He peered at her more intently, his expression full of amazement. "How do you know about Civil War weapons?"

"Oh, my dad has some old firearms at home."

"Does he collect?"

"No, he inherited his great-great-grandfather's weapons from the war. He was a corporal in Lee's Army of Northern Virginia."

She said it so perfectly, as though it wasn't a big deal, when it was the exact hook they needed to snag Baker's interest. And since it was the truth, it was that much easier for her to relate the story.

"Was he really?" Baker sounded fascinated.

"Mmhmm. We've got his service revolver, cartridge belt and forage cap as well."

"Incredible. Have you ever had them appraised? With a family history of a particular Confederate soldier attached, those things could be worth a lot of money."

"No, we've never looked into it. They're family heirlooms we wouldn't sell anyway, but one day I'd like to do more research on them. Find out where they were issued from, what battles he fought in."

"I'd be glad to put you in touch with some experts if you like."

Charlie looked back at Baker, gave a tiny smile. "Even if I can't fix your computer problem?"

"Yes, of course," he answered, all sincerity now. "I've got quite a collection myself, I've been adding to it for years now. Maybe you'd like to see it sometime."

Bingo. Jamie did a mental fist pump. Their first hint at another meeting with Baker.

Charlie didn't react, not so much of a flash in her eyes or a tensing of her muscles at the victory. God, she'd been incredible so far. Once she'd miraculously "solved" the virus problem, Baker would be hooked. "I might," she murmured, her answer and slightly coy tone perfect.

Baker stepped closer to her, gazed up at the Enfield. "It's quite extensive. One of the best in the U.S. I've had museums after me for years, trying to get me to sell them some of my pieces, including a Confederate cannon I bought from a dealer down in Louisiana."

It was both fascinating and nauseating to see Baker trying to impress Charlie with his money and prestige. Somehow Jamie managed to keep a straight face as he watched them. Baker appeared to have forgotten about him completely, which wasn't a bad thing.

"I'm sure it's wonderful, but I'm not sure it would be

appropriate," she murmured, shutting Baker down before he could continue. "Now, if you don't mind, I'd better get back to work and at least earn the outrageous down payment you agreed to give me."

With that she turned and headed back to the office without a backward glance. Leaving Baker to follow.

He was right behind her, a hound on the hunt, eyeing Charlie's ass like she was a juicy fillet he wanted to devour. "Believe me, it's already been money well spent."

****

Charlie was acutely aware of Baker's avid stare as she continued to work at his desk. He was watching her every move from his seat a few feet away, but his attention was hardly ever on what she was doing.

Everything was going well, even more smoothly than she'd hoped, but the way he watched her was making her skin crawl, a continual warning buzz at the base of her skull. Beneath the expensive suit and smooth manners, the man was a predator. And she'd just turned him down in front of another man. That had to prick his sizeable ego.

She'd known coming into this that Baker was a womanizer and that she couldn't let him get to her. She had to be friendly and interesting enough to get him to want more time with her, but not so much that she invited his advances or that she expected her to go to bed with him. Everything the agency had told her about him suggested he'd make a pass if he found her interesting enough.

Risking a glance out into the hall, she met Jamie's gaze. The subtle nod he gave her helped ease the hot ball of tension in her stomach.

Keep going. You're almost there.

All she had to do was keep cool, maintain her composure and resist Baker's…charms. Not hard to do, based on what she'd seen thus far. The man had an overinflated opinion of himself and his money.

He'd already logged into the computer before she'd ever stepped foot into his office, so she hadn't had a chance to see what kind of security or encryption he had on it. Though it had to be decent. "You said this first started last week?" she asked him.

"Sunday night, to be exact. One of my employees was in the office finishing up some work and called to alert me."

She nodded but didn't answer, busy typing commands as she assessed the extent of the virus. The one Spider had designed and Charlie's team had uploaded into his system. From what she was seeing so far, Charlie was impressed. The woman had definite style.

Baker wasn't a techie kind of guy, so when she pulled up another screen of intricate code and began to read, she knew he had no clue what he was looking at. "I'm going to go through this line by line to see if I can isolate the virus," she told him.

"Sure, go ahead. It's a pleasure to watch you work."

Eww. She'd heard some gross lines in her day, but coming from him while he sat two feet away staring at her boobs and face, it made her want to go have another shower.

It helped that Jamie had a clear visual of her from where he was positioned. If Baker tried anything and she couldn't deflect or stop it, Jamie would intervene. And what a stroke of luck, him seeing the Enfield on the wall. What she'd told Baker was true, mostly. Except that her great-great-grandfather had used a Springfield rather than an Enfield.

"Who does your programming for you?" she asked Baker a few minutes later.

"My IT department, along with the occasional outsource. Why, do you think one of them planted this?" He leaned forward, frowning.

"Can't rule it out." She kept her eyes on the screen.

"I've already got people investigating them."

Not surprising. "Good. And while you're at it, you might want to fire them and get a new IT department."

Baker blinked at her in surprise. "Why, what's wrong?"

She gestured to the screen. "There's a back door written into the original code of your operating program that allowed the hacker access to your system. It was subtle, but smart IT people should have found it. And the hacker wasn't able to hack your files, but instead input a nasty little virus out of spite. You need someone more vigilant, who's up on the latest trends if you want to stay ahead of hackers."

His brown eyes turned from thoughtful to slumberous as he regarded her. "Know anyone who might be interested?" he murmured.

The words were so loaded with innuendo she almost stopped typing. With effort, she stayed focused on her task. "I might."

He leaned back in his chair, still watching her. "So, Charlie. How did a pretty little thing like you become one of the best hackers in the world?"

She shrugged and kept typing, isolating bands of code for her to look at in more detail. "I've always liked computers and what they can do. Started out as a hobby, then I found the dark net as a teenager and haven't looked back. And that reminds me." She stopped and made herself meet his eyes. "Have you been looking in places you shouldn't with this system?"

One side of his mouth tipped upward, as though her question amused him. "No. I'm a very careful man."

"That's good." She resumed working. "Had to ask, since that's how you found me. Or rather, our contact did. And once I'm through here, I have no desire to wind up being interrogated by the Feds for helping you cover up something illegal."

"You don't need to worry about that. You won't find anything on this system that isn't entirely clean."

Yeah, we'll see about that, won't we?

There was still a chance they might find something useful to the case on Baker's office system. Even the most careful criminals screwed up. She hoped that her little lip-gloss device would transmit something that would help the team break the case open, without her having to actually go to Baker's house and try to access his personal laptop.

But if not, at least they'd know if it worked properly or not.

Nodding once, she reached into her hip pocket and pulled out the lip-gloss tube. Using a phone with the right program would have made things a lot easier, but Baker was obviously concerned about his system's security if he'd had his men take her and Jamie's phones away.

After slicking some gloss on, she subtly pressed the button to commence transmission as she slipped it back into her pocket. The device should begin transmitting files from the hard drive back to the team waiting in the mobile command center within thirty seconds.

If it worked the way it was supposed to.

Baker stayed silent as she resumed typing, pulling up page after page of code. After another twenty minutes or so, she stopped. "Ah-ha," she murmured.

"What?" Baker sat up and leaned forward, staring at the screen, close enough for her to smell the scent of his aftershave.

"Right here." She pointed to the section of suspicious code, began scrolling through it. "It's in your operating system. Not surprised the other techs you hired missed it. It's subtle. A tarantula virus. One of my personal favorites."

"What does it do?"

She steeled herself before turning her head to meet his gaze. There was no missing the calculating light there, or the desire. He wanted her, was trying to figure out how to get her. "How technical do you want me to be?"

"I want the opposite of technical."

"Okay, so basically a tarantula virus hijacks your operating system. It takes over the computer and writes the virus into each program, then erases itself from the coding before anyone can detect it."

He frowned, his attention fully on the screen now. "What's the purpose of it? Is someone trying to steal my files?"

"Maybe. Or, could be they're just screwing with you for fun. Some people get off on that kind of thing."

"Yeah, they do," he said with a hard smile that sent an icy shiver up her spine.

She typed in a few more commands, hit Enter with a flourish, and sat back. "Done."

"So, that's it?"

"That's it. I've removed the virus, and I'm running another program to make sure it's completely wiped out from the system. It'll take a few hours to run through everything. Should be good to go by around noon though. And if there are any further problems, you know how to contact me. For a fair price," she added with a cocky little grin. There was no need to stay longer in an attempt to transmit more files. This was only a test, to see if the transmitter worked the way it was supposed to.

"Excellent." Baker leaned back in his chair, a wide smile on his face, the glint in his eyes almost fascinated. "Are you by chance free tomorrow night? I'd love to take you out to dinner as a thank you. Anywhere you like, you name the place."

Could he be any less obvious? "I don't…" She slid a glance toward Jamie.

"He can come too, if it makes you feel better," Baker

said in a dismissive tone, a hint of annoyance coloring his voice.

Oh, it sure as hell does. "Maybe. James?"

From out in the hallway those amber eyes stared back at her, and if she wasn't mistaken, there was a gleam of pride there that warmed her from the inside out. "Can if you want, yeah," he answered with a half-shrug.

"Excellent." Baker stood and offered her his hand.

She hesitated only a moment before accepting it and he helped her to her feet. His palm and fingers were soft against hers. Too soft. And his grip was just a shade too possessive.

"I'll look forward to talking more about my collection with you," he murmured, then finally released her hand. She barely resisted the urge to wipe her palm on her jeans. "But first, let's take care of your payment. Believe me, you were worth every penny."

Chapter Six

Charlie let out a sigh of sheer relief when she stepped into her apartment hours later and shut the door behind her. It had been a long day and she and Jamie had just returned from a meeting with the rest of the team.

The best part about it was getting a hug from Easton when he'd walked in. She'd rather get one from Jamie, but since that wasn't going to happen, she'd had to settle for one from her brother.

Now that the initial op was over, she realized just how stressed she'd been all day. She rubbed the back of her neck and turned her head from side to side to ease the stiff muscles in her neck and shoulders. A headache throbbed in her temples.

She headed straight through to her bathroom and took two pain relievers before rummaging in her fridge for something to eat. Nothing looked the least bit appetizing, so she shut it again and headed to the bedroom instead. Her mind kept wandering back to this morning as she rummaged through the clothes she'd brought, searching for her loungewear and robe.

Everything had gone better than expected so far. Baker was definitely interested in her—well, the version of Spider he'd met today— and she'd gained at least a measure of his trust today by getting rid of the virus for him.

The man was gross, totally skeevy, but she'd have to see him again. And again, until she could get access to his laptop without him being suspicious.

The thought exhausted her even more. At the meeting the team had decided she should meet him for dinner tomorrow night with Jamie at a restaurant as planned, and see how things went. As of right now, she and Jamie were basically on their own, no more meets with the team to protect the undercover op in case Baker had people watching her or Jamie. Unless there was an emergency.

The tricky part was going to be figuring out a way to get Baker to invite her to his place in Sagaponack, so she could try and take a crack at that laptop.

For now the plan was for her to keep pulling on the weapons collection thread. They'd brainstormed several ideas at the meeting. The transmitter appeared to have worked well enough, at least from initial analysis, but it had only been able to send a small amount of files to the team while Charlie had been working.

Taylor was going over the data now to see if she could find anything of use for the case. No one was holding their breath on that count, however. Baker wouldn't be stupid enough to leave files on his criminal activity on his work server. Charlie still had to find a way to access his laptop.

Right now, she didn't even want to think about that.

The peace and quiet after such a long, stressful day was bliss. She took a hot shower, changed into her fuzzy jammies and robe, and flopped on the couch to watch some TV, thinking about what to order in for dinner.

A knock at the door a few minutes later made her groan. She got up and went to answer it, her heart skipping a beat when she saw one of Jamie's eyes peering back at her through the peephole. Laughing, she unlocked the door and pulled it open.

"I come bearing pizza and your favorite beer," he said, holding both up.

The rich smell of the tomato sauce coming from the cardboard box made her stomach growl and her mouth water. She could also use some company right now. "I can't resist that offer. Come on in."

He eyed her outfit as he stepped inside. "Ready for bed already? It's not even eight o'clock."

"Been a long day, so I made myself cozy." Thankfully the headache was beginning to ease up.

"Yeah, I know it was."

She grabbed plates and napkins from the kitchen then led the way over to the couch, took a seat on one end of it while he took the other. "How did you know this is my favorite beer, anyway?" she asked in suspicion, twisting it open. It wasn't a common brand.

"I remember you drinking it at your dad's place. Spotted some in the cooler when I was down at the liquor store on the corner and thought I'd grab it."

Shouldn't have surprised her that he'd remembered details like that. The man had serious training and didn't miss much. "Well thanks." His thoughtfulness touched her.

"You're welcome. You earned it. Great job today."

His praise sent a rush of warmth through her.

The building had been under surveillance by the team while they'd been gone, and no one had breached either apartment, so she was safe to break character here. "Thanks. Just glad everything went smoothly, and that I didn't blow our covers." She took a sip of beer, sighed as the cold, bitter brew slid down her throat. "Oh, man, that's good."

"So what did you think of him?" Jamie asked, helping himself to a slice of pizza.

She wrinkled her nose. "He's…slimy." She'd barely kept from smacking his hand away when he'd put it on the small of her back this morning.

"Yep. Asshole kept stripping you with his eyes the entire time you were working," he muttered, sounding none too happy about it.

"Ick. Can we talk about something else?"

"Sure. How's your dad doing?" He reached for a second slice.

The question surprised her. "Pretty well, all things considered." He'd suffered a debilitating stroke a few years back. His speech was slurred and one side of his body was weak but his mind was still razor sharp. "It's been harder on him since Wyatt moved in with Austen." Her eldest brother and his fiancée had renovated an old Victorian house together and were now living in it.

Jamie nodded. "Easton said that too."

He and Easton were close. Much closer than she'd realized until this op. She'd watched them together during meetings and team meals over the past few days, the way they talked and laughed together. Totally at ease with one another, like brothers.

"I've been going back at least every other weekend to visit him. I'll do a big grocery shop for him, freeze some meals and run errands, give the house a good scrubbing since he's too stubborn and cheap to hire a cleaning service. My brothers help out when they can, and my future sisters-in-law have been awesome too. Even Trinity." She glanced at him. "Have you met her yet?"

"Just once." His lips quirked, his golden-amber eyes warming with a smile. "She's unique. Mysterious," he added as he chewed.

It was hard not to stare at the way his lips moved as he chewed. Full, shockingly soft lips she remembered exactly how they'd felt on her own. Watching him now reminded her how badly she wanted to feel that delectable mouth on the rest of her body.

Mostly because it was Jamie, and a little because he posed a challenge her competitive streak demanded she keep chipping away at until she got her way.

She pushed the distracting thoughts aside. "Oh yeah. Pretty sure I still haven't scratched the surface of her, even though I try to pop over to see her and Brody about once a week or so." She'd never seen her middle brother so happy.

"You're really close to your family," he said in an almost approving tone as he reached for his own beer.

"Yeah, I am." She wanted to know more about his. It felt strange that he knew all about hers when she knew almost nothing about his, except that his parents were both originally from Mexico and now lived in Southern California. She'd asked Easton a few things about him over the past year but not too much, not wanting to seem overly curious in case it tipped her brother off that something was going on between them.

Well, *had* been going on. "My mom died when I was little and it's been just the five of us ever since. My dad made it a priority that we stick together and stay close, no matter what. And trust me, that wasn't always easy, especially after Wyatt was wounded." In the depths of his depression her eldest brother had tried to push his family away along with everyone else.

No damn way they'd been about to let that happen. Some of the run-ins she'd had with him had been epic and were now family legend, but she didn't regret a thing. Wyatt was more like his old self now than ever before.

Jamie set his beer down on the table, the muscles in his arm shifting as he moved. The man was distraction and temptation personified. "I'll bet. I'm sorry about your mom. That must have been hard, losing her when you were so young."

A pang hit her in the center of her chest. It always happened when she thought of her mom, and how grief-stricken her mom had been at the thought of leaving them behind. "Thanks. I think it's been toughest on my dad though. They'd been together forever, since high school. He's lonely but never dated anyone after she passed, and wouldn't now because of the stroke, even if another woman out there could tolerate his gruffness." She chewed a mouthful of pizza, thoughtful. "It's funny what I remember about her. I can still remember the way she smelled. Sweet, like vanilla, from her perfume."

He merely watched her as he continued to eat, so she kept talking.

"I was so young, I only have a few really clear memories of her. One Christmas dinner in particular. Her carrying my cake into the dining room on my fifth birthday. She always made each of us our favorite kind of cake from scratch for our birthdays. I remember cuddling up in bed together while she read me stories." A wistful ache swelled inside her. "Other than that, I mostly know her through pictures and stories from my dad and brothers. I wish I'd had more time to make memories with her."

"But you remember how much she loved you."

"Yes, absolutely." That's why losing her still hurt so much. She shifted on the couch, a little uncomfortable at having just revealed all that. "What about you?"

He broke eye contact, busied himself with lifting another piece of pizza from the box. "I'm close with my family too."

"You've got a sister, right?"

He nodded. "Two years older than me. We fought like crazy when we were kids, but never in front of my parents because we weren't stupid. My mom had this thing about wooden spoons. I don't know how many she went through over the years from spanking us when we deserved it, but I'm guessing it was quite a few. Only when we fought or were disrespectful though. We learned in a hurry to fight in private."

Charlie smiled, already liking the sound of his mom. "But you're close to your sister now?"

"Yeah. She's married and expecting a baby in another few months."

"So are you excited to be an uncle?" She had trouble imagining him handling a baby; he just didn't seem like the kind of guy who would be comfortable with it.

"Can't wait. If I can get the time off I'm going to be there when the baby's due."

That was so sweet, and unexpected from such an intense, hard-edged man. Tonight he was showing her a side of him she'd never known existed, and now it was even harder to keep her distance.

She had to though. She wasn't ready to give up her independence or commit to any man. She'd lived long enough doing what she was told, and putting aside everything else in her life when her brother and father needed her during their recoveries. Now she was free to do whatever she wanted and she relished the independence.

"If I had to guess, Piper and Easton will probably start a family soon after they get married." Maybe Austen and Wyatt too, which would be a trip. Trinity couldn't have kids, and Charlie wasn't sure she even wanted to, but if they wanted kids she and Brody could always adopt one day.

"Yeah, he told me. Piper's worried if they wait too much longer, she might not be able to have a baby."

Charlie stilled, the piece of pizza inches from her mouth. Easton had told him that, but not her? "Oh."

Jamie still wasn't making eye contact with her, however, and something told her he was holding back something big from her. "Must be hard, being that far away from your family all the time," she said, watching him. "I'm only a few hours away, and two of my brothers live right near D.C. but I still miss them when they're off on a mission or training op."

Another nod, still no eye contact. "We usually talk on the phone a couple times a week, but…yeah. I don't get back home as much as I'd like."

Okay, there was definitely something in his tone and expression. Guilt? "That's the great part about being from a tight-knit family though. They might drive you crazy and get all up in your business, but only because they care, and they'll always be there for you."

Jamie stopped chewing, seemed to force himself to swallow before reaching for his beer again. "Not always, which you understand better than most people."

Charlie lowered her pizza to the plate in her lap, dread gathering in the pit of her stomach at his leaden tone. "What do you mean? What's wrong?"

"My mom's sick."

Her appetite vanished. "How sick?"

Those golden-brown eyes finally lifted to hers, held. "She's dying. MS."

The pizza turned into a gelatinous lump in her stomach. "Oh my God, I'm so sorry." How had she not known this? Why had Easton never said anything?

He nodded stiffly. "We're not sure exactly how much time she has left, but she's almost at the palliative stage and she's been having trouble swallowing anything on her own for the past few days. My dad's been trying to force feed her things through a straw, to see if that helps. Soup, milkshakes, whatever he can get down her to keep her from wasting away."

Oh, that was awful. She wanted to put her arms

around him so badly but wasn't sure he'd let her and something warned her not to cross the invisible barrier between them even in that innocent way. "And instead of being there, you're stuck here with me on this op."

One side of his mouth curled upward in a wry grin. "Well. Not the worst thing I've ever had to do in the line of duty."

"Gee, thanks," she teased, playing along as he attempted to lighten the mood.

He chuckled, then sobered. "Nah, I'd go crazy sitting at her bedside, watching her slowly waste away."

He said it in a dismissive way, but his guilt was clear. And based on what he'd just told her, there was no way he wouldn't be there for his family if they needed him.

"At least this op gives me something else to focus on for the time being. And I'll be honest, I like being the one to watch your back."

Charlie didn't know what to say to that, and a sudden lump had formed in her throat anyhow. She couldn't let him know how much his words melted her.

Jamie blew out a hard breath. "So let's hope Baker gives us what we need sooner rather than later."

"Yes, let's hope." She slid her plate onto the coffee table, feeling a little sick to her stomach at the bombshell Jamie had dropped. "Does Easton know?"

"Yeah. He's been great throughout this whole thing. He gets it."

That was good. At least Jamie felt comfortable talking to him about it when he needed someone. But she would love to be the one he turned to instead.

You don't want strings, remember? Flings don't confide their deepest feelings to each other. You can't have it both ways.

Annoyed, she reached for her beer, took a sip while she contemplated him. For some reason she'd been sure she had him all figured out, but now she realized she barely knew him at all. He had a lot more depth than she'd ever given him credit for, and she was sorry she hadn't realized it until now. "You wanna talk about it more?"

"Not really."

"Okay."

He chomped down on his pizza for the next few minutes, but she could tell the situation with his mom was eating at him. "It sucks for my mom, but I feel the worst for my dad," he finally said after a long pause. "They've been together thirty-four years now. They were first loves, met when they were teenagers. He'll be totally lost without her."

"That's so sweet." And bittersweet, now that his dad was going to lose her. "My parents were high school sweethearts." She fiddled with the label on the bottle, peeling the corner of it away from the condensation-damp glass to keep her hands busy.

This conversation was edging them firmly toward friend territory and though it was emotionally risky for her, she didn't want to avoid it or pull back. Something about putting her safety in his hands today and now him opening up to her had shifted the dynamic of their relationship.

She wasn't sure if that was good or bad. All she knew was, it felt good to talk to him. For all the heat and passion simmering between them, they still didn't know each other that well yet.

"I remember my mom being sick, but not really how it felt," she went on when he stayed quiet. "I've got just a vague recollection of anxiety and fear as she got worse. Then one day my dad didn't take us all up to the hospital in the afternoon like he usually did. She was gone. Just gone. And I still regret not being there to say goodbye and tell her I loved her one last time." Chest tight, she looked over at him, found him watching her with that steady, honeyed gaze. "Trust me when I tell you, you don't want to live with that same regret."

"No. I've been going home to visit whenever I can, even if it's just for a day or two over the weekend. And when it gets close to the end, I'll take a leave of absence if I have to. There's no way I wouldn't be there when she goes."

She hated that he was dealing with something so devastating. Couldn't believe she hadn't known any of this until now.

Because it was none of your business. "Good. That's good," she murmured, not knowing what else to say.

"We can change the subject now. Didn't mean to be a downer."

"No, I'm glad you told me. And hey, bonus that it took my mind off Baker for a little while."

The edges of his mouth lifted a little. "Then I'm glad."

She curled into the corner of the couch, drew her knees up and tucked her hands between them. "Is that why you're so set on all or nothing with me?"

His gaze jumped to hers, his surprise clear at the abrupt shift in topic. "Doesn't matter. You made it clear you're not interested, and besides, now we're working together."

"And I'm Easton's sister."

A grin tugged at his mouth. "Yeah, and that too."

But that wasn't as important as the other reasons. Interesting.

He was still such a mystery to her in so many ways. "So while we're on the subject, what's so bad about something light and short term, hypothetically speaking?"

His expression was equal parts wary and heated. "I won't settle anymore. I know what I want, and I won't take anything less."

And he still wanted her, but only if she was all in. The tantalizing possibility sent a thrill rushing through her veins. "Why me? You don't really know me."

"I know enough." He lifted a shoulder, his muscles bunching under the dark T-shirt. "We've got a lot in common."

She lifted an eyebrow. "Such as?"

"You grew up in a military family so you understand the lifestyle, what makes guys like us tick."

"Somewhat, yeah."

"And you know just how short life can be."

Their mothers. Wyatt. Her father. No one knew how long they had on this earth. Nothing was guaranteed. "Yes," she said softly.

"So why the no strings stance, then? What are you so afraid of?"

The question threw her so much, she immediately scowled. "It's got nothing to do with me being afraid."

He gave her a look that said he didn't believe her. "Then why?"

Still scowling, she floundered for a response, which was totally unlike her. But no one had ever asked her that before, and she'd never questioned her reasoning, much less examined it. "I just...don't like being told what to do with my life."

"Uh huh." His tone called total bullshit.

What are you so afraid of?

She'd tried to dismiss it out of hand, but the question was still resonating inside her like the hum of a tuning fork. Powerful and specific.

Was she afraid? Just the idea seemed laughable, and yet... There was something about it that spoke to her.

She'd never really thought about it before, but after seeing what her father had gone through after losing her mother... God, maybe Jamie was right.

She vividly remembered deciding the day of her mother's funeral that she didn't ever want to experience that kind of pain. So had she subconsciously tried to avoid a committed relationship thus far out of a sense of self-preservation? Trying to avoid being hurt by remaining emotionally distant from the men she'd dated in the past?

It fit. More than that, it rang true inside her, shocking her more than the initial question had.

Jamie continued to watch her with those eyes that saw far too much, waiting for a response. God, how the hell had he seen so deeply inside her when she hadn't even been aware of it herself until a moment ago?

Shaken but refusing to let him know it, she finally found her voice, put a sarcastic edge into it so he wouldn't know how his words had affected her. "You forgot one other thing we have in common: stubbornness. That means we'd probably fight a lot."

His answering smile was slow, and hot enough to melt her insides. "Then I guess we'd make up a lot too. Unless you hold grudges?"

She'd been known to hold a grudge or two. "Depends on what you did to make me mad."

He chuckled and wiped his hands on the paper napkin she'd given him. Lean, strong hands, the bronzed skin nicked in places. What she wouldn't give to feel them running all over her naked body right now.

She eyed him, wishing she could see inside his head and understand why he was so set on all or nothing. She didn't like feeling emotionally naked like this when he still kept so much from her. "So that's your reason? You won't settle."

"Mostly."

"So there's more?" she pressed, wanting to put them on a more even keel, emotionally speaking.

"Yeah, there's more."

She waited a beat for him to continue, but he didn't, and she couldn't help but laugh softly. "I hate that you're leaving me hanging."

He merely smiled, the smug edge to it telling her it

was intentional and that he was enjoying it. "Gotta keep you guessing."

Oh really? "All part of your plan to keep me interested?"

"Maybe." Before she could think of a smart comeback, he pushed up from the couch. "Well. Big day tomorrow. Better let you get a good night's sleep."

I'd sleep better after I've had you inside me. She scrambled to her feet and followed him to the door, wishing things were different. That he would drop the insistence on the commitment issue, stay the night and put an end to the longing that had tortured her for so long. "You want the rest of the pizza?"

"Nah. I know you love cold pizza for breakfast."

She frowned. "And just how do you know that?" How did he seem to know so damn much about her?

He paused at the door, hand on the knob, that long, hard body a mere two feet away from her. "I know a lot more about you than you realize."

Easton. Had to be. "I'll save you some."

"No thanks. I'm a plain old coffee for breakfast kind of guy. If you're up early enough, we can go grab some at the café on the corner before the meeting." His gaze slid over her face, coming to rest on her mouth for a moment before returning to her eyes.

Tingles of heat spread across her skin as she remembered the way he kissed. Dominant, yet seductive. Scorching hot, yet holding part of himself back. She wanted to see him unleash the wild hunger and need she sensed in him.

Silent laughter lit the depths of his eyes, as though he knew his presence was tormenting her. "But since we both know you're not a morning person, I won't hold my breath on that one."

With that teasing —and accurate—admonishment, he walked out of her apartment.

Charlie locked the door behind him, her entire body aching for his touch. She laid her forehead against the door and let out a frustrated groan.

Jamie wasn't the only one who wouldn't settle. She wanted him and no one else, but he refused to give into her.

That left her in a hell of a situation, because the man was slowly driving her crazy and there was no relief in sight.

****

Jamie gave up trying to force himself to sleep an hour later and rolled over onto his back in his empty bed. No matter how much he tried, he couldn't stop thinking about Charlie, and the unrelieved hunger between them that threatened to burn a hole in his gut.

She'd been so real with him tonight, so relaxed, right up until he'd pushed her about what was holding her back from giving them an honest chance. It had taken an act of will not to take her face between his hands and kiss her until she couldn't stand up.

He didn't know what the hell she was so afraid of. According to Easton, she hadn't had any bad breakups that he knew of, or had her heart broken by any of the guys she'd dated. So what was it? Life was way too unpredictable and too damn short to spend it holding back, and she knew it as well as he did.

It was torture, knowing she wanted him and that she was just on the other side of the wall. But he couldn't give in. The stakes were too high. She was too important.

His cock was rock hard beneath the sheet, aching, just from thinking about her. Since it wasn't going away anytime soon and he'd never be able to sleep with his body wound so tight, he gave in and slid a hand down his stomach to grasp it.

He closed his eyes, fell into one of his favorite fantasies about Charlie that he'd dreamed up almost a year ago. She was as naked as him, kneeling between his spread feet, dark eyes aglow with hunger as she stared up into his eyes. Her tongue darted across her lush lower lip as she watched him stroke himself, her fingers flexing restlessly on the backs of his thighs.

So many nights he'd thought about her this way, spinning fantasies about what it would be like with her. She burned with a passion that was impossible to ignore.

In his mind's eye, he gripped the base of his cock with one hand and bunched the other in the thick, cool fall of her hair, tugging her closer. Charlie leaned forward, eyes heavy-lidded as she parted those soft lips, slowly enveloping the swollen, sensitive crown in the scalding warmth of her mouth.

He shuddered, hips arching off the mattress, pleasure rocketing up his spine and pulling his balls up tight against his body. So good. Always so intense with her.

Dream Charlie made a soft sound in the back of her throat as she closed around him, her warm tongue swirling around him while she sucked at the head as though he was a favorite treat she intended to savor. Sensation burst through him, tingling across every nerve ending.

His muscles strained, his thighs and belly twitching as he reached the edge. The sound of his rough breathing was harsh in the quiet. He stroked faster, imagined it was her luscious mouth working him.

Sucking. Enjoying the attempt at breaking his control.

Fuck.

A ragged sound dragged up from the center of his chest as the sensation red-lined. He squeezed his eyes shut, locked his jaw to keep from calling out her name in the darkness. It echoed in his head instead as the orgasm swept over him and he came all over his belly.

Charlie. Charlie...

Breathing hard, he groaned and collapsed back against the sheet, sticky and sweaty.

And oddly unrelieved despite the release he'd just given himself. Because he was sick of making do with his own hand when she was right there for the taking.

With a harsh sigh he swung his legs over the side of the bed and headed to the bathroom to clean up. Tomorrow was hurtling toward them way too fast, and there was nothing he could do to resolve the distance between them until this job was over.

Chapter Seven

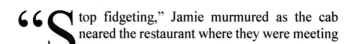

"Stop fidgeting," Jamie murmured as the cab neared the restaurant where they were meeting Baker.

Charlie pushed out a breath. "Right." She wiped her palms over the skirt of her dress and squared her shoulders, the motion pushing her breasts out even more.

The muscles in his stomach grabbed. It was torture, being this close and not able to touch her. Even after resorting to using his own hand last night to take the edge off, he still hadn't slept worth a damn. He'd come so close to kissing her at her door last night, but thank God he'd listened to logic and resisted the temptation.

She'd been so real with him, so open compared to the past week. During that conversation, he'd fallen a little more in love with her. Much more and he'd be in deep trouble. A woman as strong and determined as Charlie could shred him if he didn't stand firm on his demands.

Once this was all over, he had a choice. Walk away, or do everything in his power to convince her to give them a shot.

He already knew the former wasn't going to be an option.

His phone buzzed, yanking him back to the present. A text message from one of his teammates.

"Logan and Taylor are already inside." His teammate and a female agent friend of Charlie's were at the restaurant posing as a couple out to dinner to provide extra surveillance, since Jamie couldn't maintain his normal level of vigilance without raising suspicion. They didn't think Baker was suspicious that anything was going on, but they weren't leaving it to chance either. Baker was going to be cautious as well, so they expected him to be watching them. "Baker too."

"Okay."

The driver parked at the curb in front of the restaurant. Jamie paid him and glanced toward Charlie, who had her game face firmly in place. "Ready?"

"Ready." She reached for the door handle and climbed out in that sexy as hell electric blue dress, and it was all he could do to tear his eyes off the miles and miles of bare leg in front of him.

The soft fabric of the dress flowed around her hips as she moved, ending halfway up her thighs. She wore the same black leather jacket as yesterday, giving the otherwise feminine outfit an edge that matched Spider's persona. Spiky black high-heels accentuated the muscles in her calves and thighs, made him imagine peeling that dress off her and leaving her in whatever she had on underneath as he laid her down in the center of his bed.

He wouldn't say a word while he picked up one foot in his hands, letting her anticipate what he would do. If and when he did take her to bed, he wanted full control. Wanted to shatter any illusions she stubbornly clung to and show her that he was unlike anyone she'd ever been with before.

He'd look straight into her eyes as he slowly

unbuckled the strap around her lower leg, slide the shoe off and settle his mouth on the delicate bones of her inner ankle.

He'd watch her eyes widen in surprise, drink in her gasp of startled pleasure while he pressed his thumbs into the arch of her foot with firm pressure and sucked on each of her toes before nibbling his way up the length of her leg to the soft, secret flesh between.

Jamie swallowed and shifted in his seat, the fit of his pants suddenly tighter than they had been a moment ago. Charlie looked amazing. Baker was going to start drooling the second he saw her.

Shoving back the territorial and protective need to put a hand on her back or waist, Jamie walked beside her up to the front door. The restaurant Baker had chosen was upscale and exclusive, the kind of place where a salad cost as much as the bill for an entire meal somewhere else.

At any rate, this place was way above the pay grade for a personal trainer like Jamie's cover. No doubt that wasn't a coincidence. Baker loved to throw around his weight and money, always needing his ego stroked by letting everyone around him know how rich and important he was.

And he probably expected Charlie to stroke other parts of him at some point later on, too. For sure the asshole had been fantasizing about it.

The thought made Jamie clench his jaw. He didn't like that bastard even thinking about touching her, let alone imagining her in bed.

Charlie glanced at him when he opened the door for her, and paused, her eyebrows rising. "You okay? You look ready to kill something."

Shit. He needed to get it together. This was an important op. "Nah, I'm good." He smoothed out his expression, glanced around to get his bearings in the crowded restaurant while trying not to look too alert. The team had their back and he trusted them to have their six. But some things were deeply ingrained.

A smiling hostess came over and escorted them to their table. He stayed a few paces behind Charlie, spotted Logan and Taylor at a table on the other side of the room, briefly made eye contact with his teammate before searching for Baker.

The man was dressed in a light gray suit, standing at their table near the back of the restaurant, his avid gaze locked on Charlie as they approached. Baker didn't even try to be subtle about the way he was checking her out, waiting until the last possible moment to tear his eyes from her breasts and drag them up to her face.

You don't care. Let him look all he wants because it doesn't bother you, Charlie's just your neighbor, nothing more.

The reminder didn't help. At all.

"Charlie," Baker said, taking her hand in his when they reached the table and raising it to his lips. "You look incredible."

Jamie had to give her credit for not yanking her hand free of his slimy grasp. "Thanks," she murmured.

Baker spared him a glance. "James."

"Hey." *I'd like to punch that oily smirk right off your face.*

Dismissing him, Baker pulled out Charlie's chair for her—directly across the table from him, probably so he could leer at her to his heart's content—then sat down. "I took the liberty of ordering us some red wine. Would you care for some?" he asked her.

"No thanks. I'm a beer gal."

An amused smile curved his mouth. "Of course." He signaled the waiter.

Jamie cast a quick glance around them. He didn't spot any familiar faces from the files he'd been studying, men thought to be involved with Baker in his business of cleaning dirty money for the cartel and other criminal organizations.

"How's your system working? Any more trouble?" Charlie asked.

"No, everything's running like a well-oiled machine now," Baker said. "You performed a minor miracle yesterday."

No, the miracle was that Charlie could sit here and do this without cringing.

"Glad I could help," was all she said, smiling her thanks at the waiter who brought over her beer. "Did you want anything?" she asked Jamie, pulling her lip-gloss from her purse and applying it to her lush mouth. She'd been really good about remembering to use it every so often, so it wouldn't seem odd when she used it around Baker.

"I'll have a beer too," he told the waiter, enjoying the slightly awkward lapse caused by calling attention to Baker's lack of manners.

"You'll pardon me if I tend to monopolize Charlie's attention tonight," Baker said with a tight smile as the waiter walked away. "It's not often I have the pleasure of meeting such a beautiful and talented woman." His gaze shifted back to Charlie, gleaming with a borderline predatory interest that made Jamie's hackles rise.

"It's all right. It's not like he's enjoying himself anyhow," Charlie said with a laugh. "Pretty sure he'd rather be back in his apartment right now, on the couch watching a ballgame."

"Well perhaps after we get to know each other better tonight, you'll feel safe enough to meet me unaccompanied next time, and he can stay at home," Baker murmured.

"Maybe," she said, and left it at that.

Jamie stared at him across the table. *No way in hell, asshole.*

But Baker had already launched into a new topic of conversation with Charlie and didn't even notice. Jamie internally shook his head at his predicament and sat back in his chair, resigned to enduring having to watch Baker attempt to woo the woman Jamie was falling in love with for the rest of the night.

He couldn't freaking wait until they nailed this son of a bitch for money laundering and whatever else he'd dirtied his hands with, and put Baker in jail where he belonged.

****

"Wow, talk about a fifth wheel."

Special Agent Taylor Kennedy glanced up from her plate in surprise to look at the man seated across the table. "What do you mean?" she asked.

They'd barely spoken since they'd sat down a few minutes ago, the awkwardness threatening to edge her nervousness into full-blown anxiety she was struggling not to show. She would so much rather be back at the hotel working on the files Charlie had transmitted today from Pinnacle Group, instead of here on the world's most uncomfortable fake date of all time.

Not that Special Agent Logan Granger seemed to notice.

By way of answer he hid a smile behind the rim of his coffee cup and looked subtly toward Charlie and Jamie's table near the back of the restaurant. He'd asked for this table against the exterior wall and had positioned himself on the far side of it for the best view of Jamie and Charlie.

"Dude's completely ignoring Jamie's existence. And from the looks of it I think he plans to keep doing that all night. Not that I blame him," he added, lowering his mug and leaning back in his chair, the motion pulling his cream-colored dress shirt taut over his muscular chest and shoulders. "She's a hell of a lot nicer to look at than Rodriguez's ugly mug."

Taylor tore her gaze away from him, resisting the urge to turn around and see for herself. "Is he alone?" Tucking a strand of hair behind her ear, she tried once again to quell the nerves jumping in her stomach. She'd worn contacts instead of her glasses, and they were already bugging her eyes, making them feel dry and uncomfortable.

She kept telling herself there was nothing for her to be nervous about. She was a professional, and they were only here to appear like a couple out on a date, so Logan could keep watch for other players Baker might have brought along. Coming here to spy on Baker didn't bother her, and if anything did happen, she had some training.

No, the problem was the man sitting across from her.

Logan was apparently FAST Bravo's newest member, and a former DEA undercover agent. With his reddish-brown beard and broad shoulders, all he needed was a plaid flannel shirt and an axe to complete his rugged, outdoorsy image. He was also huge, his size and obvious strength secretly unsettling her.

It didn't happen too often anymore, but every once in a while being around a large man would set her inner radar buzzing. Something ingrained in her long ago. Combined with her discomfort about being here, sitting this close to him stirred up ghosts from her past she'd thought long buried.

Apparently she'd been wrong. They were alive and well, still lurking around in her frightened twelve-year-old subconscious.

The realization shamed her. She should be stronger than that. Strong enough to banish the memories and lock them away in a place where they could never escape again. God knew she'd done her best to vanquish them.

"Everything's cool. They're alone." Logan snorted. "And buddy can't seem to drag his eyes off her anyway. Well, her boobs, to be precise."

Gross. Taylor wrinkled her nose. Men like Baker thought they could have or do anything to a woman they wanted, simply because they were rich. They were disgusting pigs and she couldn't wait for Charlie to finally gain access to that laptop so they could find something to nail his privileged ass with and put him away for a long time. "I feel bad for her."

"She's handling it like a boss." His tone was full of admiration.

"I'm just glad she's not alone with that guy." Charlie was one of the first people she'd met after moving to D.C. and they'd become good friends. They went out to movies together or out to dinner a couple times a month. She'd tried to get Charlie interested in joining her book club a while back, but that hadn't gone over too well.

Taylor was worried about her. Charlie might be mentally tough and know how to handle a firearm, but she was a civilian employee, not a trained field agent. Taylor had tried to volunteer for this op but the head of the taskforce had wanted Charlie because of her computer expertise and because she had the look Baker liked best.

And you think you're stronger than her? A full-fledged special agent who's nervous just sitting across from Logan?

Sometimes her inner voice was damn mean.

But it was almost always dead on.

Wincing inside, Taylor reached for her stemmed water glass and took a sip, her gaze on her plate once again. It helped to avoid looking at Logan whenever possible. "I guess it's a good thing he seems interested in her."

"You not hungry?" he asked, glancing at her nearly untouched salad.

She'd poked around at it for the last five minutes, basically moving pieces of lettuce and fruit around on her plate but not eating. "Not really." To give her hand something to do, she picked up her fork and scooped up some dressing-glossed greens, put it in her mouth and chewed.

Logan shifted in his chair. She stilled at the movement, even stopped chewing for a second, watching him. "You okay?" he asked.

She swallowed and nodded despite the sudden restriction in her throat, gave a wry smile as she forked up another bite. "Yes. Sorry. Bet you wish you'd taken someone else out to dinner, huh."

"You're fine."

"Been a while since I've done this," she said, completely willing to laugh at herself.

"Yeah? How long."

She considered it for a moment. "Can't remember."

Months at least. The last date she'd been on was with a guy she'd met through an online dating site, and it had been a total disaster. She'd wound up texting Charlie an hour in, begging for an excuse to bolt. Charlie had come through for her, calling with a fake family emergency.

"I'm a lot more comfortable spending time with my spreadsheets and all the paperwork that comes with an investigation, rather than being out on a date," she finished. *Even if it's a fake one.*

Though there were a lot worse assignments than having to endure dinner out with a trained and ruggedly good-looking guy like Logan.

"It doesn't show at all," he deadpanned, somehow managing to keep a straight face. He relaxed his posture, rested both arms on the chair's armrests, as though he somehow guessed it made her more comfortable when she could see his hands. "Nothing's gonna happen here tonight, I promise. Might as well relax and enjoy a nice dinner together on the company's dime, right?" He even smiled at her, a non-threatening, teasing smile meant to put her at ease that she found far more attractive than she wanted to.

She returned the smile, even though it was a little forced. Her cheeks flushed slightly, partly from self-consciousness, and partly because she felt so damn awkward. She'd never been out with a man like Logan. "Sure."

He nodded and settled back into his chair, his sharp gaze sweeping casually over the restaurant. It was fascinating to watch him take everything in, see him catalogue things that most people missed. No doubt he knew exactly how many tables were in the room, where all the exits were. And for sure he would always keep sight of Baker, even when he wasn't looking directly at the man.

Those blue-green eyes came back to her a moment later, taking her by surprise. "So, Taylor. You're from Houston, right?"

She hastily swallowed her mouthful of salad. She wasn't such a dork that she couldn't make polite conversation. For a little while. "Yes. You?"

"Maine."

"Ah."

He cocked his head. "Ah, what?"

She flushed harder. "Nothing," she said, waving a hand. Okay, maybe she was a dork.

"No, what?"

It probably sounded stupid to him. "I just...you remind me a bit of a lumberjack. So being from Maine fits my image of you, that's all."

He quirked an eyebrow. "A lumberjack, huh? Not a cowboy or a Scottish highlander? That's disappointing. But yeah, I've spent some time swinging an axe back home, so I guess that's accurate."

Oh, hell. Unbidden, an image of him popped into her mind: shirtless, standing outside a cabin in the woods while he slammed an axe down on the end of a log, the muscles now hidden beneath the snug fit of his dress shirt revealed in all their sweat-slicked glory.

She grabbed for her water glass, nearly knocked it over in her haste to gulp down a sip and wet her suddenly dry throat. How the hell freaking long was this dinner going to take, anyway?

Taylor mentally scowled as she drained the rest of her water. Why had she agreed to do this? She had spreadsheets to get back to and numbers to crunch, alone back in her hotel room, where she'd be comfortable.

Spreadsheets never made her feel stupid or awkward. And numbers didn't lie or try to deceive the way people did. When she was with her paperwork, she was in her element.

Paperwork *understood*.

But there was no reprieve in the near future. Stuck in this hoity-toity restaurant with the hot and rugged man across from her, she was about as far out of her element as a woman could get.

****

Dean kept his hand on the small of Charlie's back as he walked her to the front door of the restaurant. Her beefcake pseudo-bodyguard followed, his expression bored. But he wasn't fooling anyone, least of all Dean.

There was definitely something going on between James and Charlie. Maybe they hadn't acted on it yet, or maybe one or both of them hadn't even acknowledged it, but there was definitely an attraction between them.

It only made Dean want to take Charlie from him more.

He had money. Lots of money. He could show her

and give her things James never could on a personal trainer's salary. According to the guy keeping tabs on James for him, James wasn't even that successful. Barely had any clients.

What the hell Charlie saw in him besides a lot of muscle, Dean didn't know. And if the idiot was too stupid to make a move on her, it was his own fault if Dean took her out from under his nose.

He collected her coat from the restaurant employee, helped her shrug it on, the scent of leather mixing pleasantly with her light, slightly exotic perfume. Dinner had gone well, and she seemed as intelligent as he'd hoped. He'd have to move carefully with this one. She was just wary enough to pose a challenge.

And Dean loved the thrill of the hunt, especially when the prize came wrapped in such a delectable female body.

All throughout dinner he'd fantasized about the various things that could happen when he got her alone in his office. His favorite was of him sprawled in the leather chair behind his desk while she knelt in front of him, unzipped his pants and sucked him off right there. Blood rushed to his groin, excitement leaping inside him.

"Thank you," she murmured, and carefully stepped away out of reach. Cool, guarded.

Street smart. She'd avoided his touch a few times before, but it didn't bother Dean. It simply made him hungrier for the chase.

Her big, dark eyes lifted to his, the sharp intelligence there yet another turn-on. Intelligent women were hard to come by. "Thanks for the contact info on your weapons expert. Next time I go home I'll get the serial number on the Enfield and get in touch with him."

He could do better than that, and he wanted to see her again anyway, as soon as possible. "Are you free this weekend?" He didn't even know where James was right now, and didn't care. As far as Dean was concerned, the man didn't exist.

She paused in the act of pushing a lock of shiny brown hair over her shoulder. "Maybe. Why?"

Such a cautious little thing. They had more in common than she realized. "I have a house out in The Hamptons." But he was sure she already knew that. There was no way she hadn't looked him up well before she'd arrived at his office yesterday morning.

Another reason why it surprised him that she wasn't more open to his so far subtle advances. Most other women would have jumped at the chance to sleep with him if they thought there was some kind of financial benefit in it for them. If she was playing hard to get, it was not only working, she was also a better actress than he'd ever come across.

"Sagaponack, to be exact," he continued. "I'm having an exclusive get-together tomorrow night, and I've already invited my weapons expert friend. You could talk to him there, and then I'd also have the chance to show you my collection in private."

He only extended the invitation because his people had already checked her and James out. Tim had found exactly what Dean had already been told—Charlie was a website designer and James a personal trainer. They lived next door to one another in an older apartment building in Brooklyn, and had for the past several months. Neither one of them made much money, so evidently Charlie didn't use her hacking skills to further herself financially.

Dean found that interesting. And intriguing. The amount he had paid her yesterday was likely as much as she made in an entire year after taxes with her website business, maybe more.

Giving Charlie a glimpse of life in The Hamptons would show her the finer things in life, might warm her up to the idea of having sex with him. He'd prefer to have her willing and not have to resort to drugging her.

So far she'd been polite yet distant with him, but he wasn't worried. Everyone had a price. He'd seen firsthand how knowledgeable she was at her work. If necessary he could recruit her to do some personal jobs for him or his clients, if he dangled the right offer in front of her. Or maybe she had no further use to him, in terms of business. He hadn't decided yet.

What he did know was that he wanted her more than he'd wanted any other woman in a long time, and he was enjoying the hunt. There was something about her that tested him at the same time as it piqued his interest.

She was strong, a little cocky, and he liked that. He was tired of women submitting to his sexual whims simply because he had money, or because he paid them.

Or because they were afraid not to.

Something told him Charlie would never do any of those things. No, she wouldn't give in easily. She might even fight him if he forced her.

Lust shot through him like a cannon blast, swelling his cock even more. What would it take to make her give in? What was her breaking point?

With a few drinks in her he might be able to seduce her outright. If not, he could resort to other measures. He'd wait and see how things went first. "Well?" he prompted.

She glanced over at James and Dean barely stopped himself from rolling his eyes. "Yes, he can come too if you want." But if he did, Dean would make sure he kept Charlie all to himself. His security agents were well paid for their loyalty and discretion. They would keep James occupied if necessary and deal with whatever happened to Charlie, no questions asked.

At James's annoyed and bored half-shrug, Charlie turned back to Dean. "What time tomorrow?"

He hid a smile, already anticipating how tomorrow

night would go if he could get her alone for a while. "Five. Do you have a cocktail dress?"

"No, but it just so happens that I can afford to buy one now." Her little half-smile made him impatient for tomorrow afternoon to arrive.

"I'll buy one for you, and have it delivered tomorrow afternoon."

"Thank you, but no. You're technically buying it anyway, since I'll be spending some of yesterday's earnings on it. Besides, it's been a while since I had a girls' day with my bestie. She loves to shop."

He wanted to push to at least send a car for her and her friend, but held back. Being too forceful right now might scare her off. He could send Tim to follow her and her friend tomorrow. "All right."

After writing down his address for her, he walked her out the front door and to the curb, James somewhere behind them. He flagged down a cab for her and opened her door, admiring the length of bare thigh she flashed him as she slipped into the backseat.

Those legs would feel so good wrapped around his hips while he plunged in and out of her.

"See you tomorrow," he murmured, then shut the door before she could answer.

When he straightened, his gaze collided with James's, who stood on the other side of the cab, watching him. Almost in warning, but not quite. Dean held his stare, not the least bit intimidated. "I look forward to seeing you both tomorrow."

James climbed into the cab without a word.

Dean's phone rang as the cab pulled away. A delighted smile spread across his face and warmth filled him when he saw who the caller was. "Madeline. How's my best girl doing?" His eleven-year-old niece was the light of his life, so pure and innocent. He would continue to protect her with every resource available to him as long as he lived. And if any man dared defile or hurt her, they would pay. Dearly.

"Fine. Are you still going to have me over this weekend?"

Shit, he'd been so preoccupied with his plans for Charlie, he'd completely forgotten about promising to have Mads over. "Absolutely. How about you come out on Sunday afternoon?" By then his staff would have cleaned up from the party, and whatever had happened with Charlie. "We'll go out on the boat together, then have some dinner after. Any place you want, you pick. I'll send the helicopter for you." She loved it when he did that.

"Yay! Just me?"

He could just picture the excitement dancing in her big blue eyes at having her favorite uncle all to herself, without her mom there. "Just you." He loved spoiling her.

"I can't wait! What time will the pilot be here?"

"I'll text you and let you know. Bring the dress I bought you last time, in case we go somewhere fancy."

"Okay. I can't wait to tell Mom! Love you, bye."

"Love you too, sweet pea." He ended the call, watching Charlie's cab as it turned the corner and disappeared from view.

She'd be his tomorrow. One way or the other. He couldn't decide which was better, for her to come to him willingly, or for her to force his hand.

Dean smiled to himself as he waited for the valet to bring his car around, already planning what he'd do once he got her alone at the party.

Chapter Eight

By the time they made it back to the apartment building, Jamie was hanging onto his sanity by a thread. A thin one.

Anger and possessiveness swirled inside him, pushing him to the edge of his control.

Throughout the two-hour dinner, he'd been forced to sit there and endure watching Baker doing his best to charm and entice Charlie, without being able to do a damn thing about it. Had to sit there and pretend not to care every time Baker touched her hand or leaned in too close.

She'd done fine, played the part of a reluctant woman slowly warming to a seemingly charming man. It turned his stomach to remember it.

They may have gotten the all-important invite to his house tomorrow night because of it, but it came with a price. A price that was slowly eating away at Jamie's insides like acid.

Given the way Baker had been flirting with her tonight, the man was definitely going to try to put the moves on her tomorrow, and Jamie had a bad feeling he wouldn't be there to stop it. There was no way Baker would let Jamie into his private office or anywhere near the laptop, so Charlie would have to go in alone.

It tore him to shreds to think of sending her in there by herself. If anything went wrong, he was her first line of defense. But he might not even be able to fucking get to her.

Every instinct Jamie possessed screamed at him not to let her do it. He had no idea how close he could get when she went into that office, but even just outside the room was too far this time if Baker locked the door.

The whole idea was making him insane. If an emergency arose, Jamie had to alert the backup team with an emergency beacon set into his watch. Easton, Logan and Taylor would be waiting in a vehicle close by, ready to extract them, but he and Charlie had to make it to the rendezvous point on their own first.

He forced himself to take a deep breath, ignoring the sideways glances Charlie was sending his way from beside him in the back seat. He knew what he'd signed up for, understood what they needed to do and the risks associated with it.

But now he couldn't handle Charlie being in that kind of danger. Of likely having to withstand Baker's advances alone, and maybe worse if he got aggressive. Physically she was no match for him.

A queasy sensation twisted his stomach.

He walked a step or two behind her as they made their way up to the front door of the apartment building, keeping up the pretense of their cover story even though he was almost certain no one had followed them here.

He'd had the cab driver take a circuitous route from the restaurant, giving Jamie time to make sure they hadn't attracted a tail. He hadn't spotted anything to suggest they had, but just in case he'd missed something, he'd insisted they get out and walk through a crowded coffee shop and out the back before taking another cab here.

The back of his neck might not be tingling, but Baker knew where they lived and would absolutely have someone watching them at least part time.

Two steps from the front door, his cell vibrated in his pants pocket. He pulled it out, read the text from Logan, who'd followed them here in another cab and checked in with the surveillance team.

All clear.

He put the phone away without answering, anxious to get inside and lock the world out for the rest of the night. He seriously didn't know how Logan had done undercover work for as long as he had. Jamie had only been on this op for a few days and he was ready to split apart at the seams from stressing about Charlie and trying to repress his feelings for her.

Man, he'd give anything right now for them both to be back in D.C., him with his team, training with the guys.

He walked into the elevator with her, stuffed his hands into his pockets where he could curl them into fists without giving himself away. In the silence, Charlie glanced over at him with a questioning look but didn't say anything, then went back to staring at the closed doors in front of them.

That dress was killing him. Not being able to stop this was killing him. Not being able to *touch* her was killing him.

Cables groaned and shuddered as the elevator reached their floor. Jamie clenched his jaw, unable to stop his mind from spinning. He'd never struggled like this on a job before.

But none of the jobs had ever involved a woman he'd fallen in love with.

Thinking of what could happen tomorrow night at the party was slowly ripping him apart inside. How the hell was he going to protect her if he couldn't be in the office with her?

He had to find a way. He'd promised her and Easton. Could never live with himself if Baker assaulted her.

He studied Charlie's profile, aching inside. She was so strong and loyal and proud. Imagining Baker wounding or breaking her spirit tomorrow night made him want to smash his fist into the elevator wall.

The elevator doors opened. It smelled like someone on their floor was cooking something Italian. Their footsteps were silent on the hallway carpet as Charlie walked ahead of him. Her door loomed up ahead in the middle of the hallway. In just another few seconds she'd unlock it and disappear inside her apartment.

His pulse thudded hard in his ears, seeming to grow louder with every step. He didn't want to let her go. Needed to touch her, kiss her, stake some kind of claim on her once and for all so that even if Baker did put his filthy hands on her tomorrow, maybe the memory of Jamie's touch would erase it. Or at least make it easier for her to bear somehow.

She put her key into her lock, paused to glance at him. "Have I done something wrong?"

"No," he bit out. She'd been perfect so far.

Her expression hardened at his tone and she turned away. "Okay. Goodnight."

When she stepped inside and started to shut the door, something inside him snapped.

He slapped a palm against the door to stop it from closing in his face. Her eyes jerked up to his, widened as she stared at him through the gap.

Before the logical part of his brain could take over he barged in and locked the door behind him. Charlie backed away a few feet and stopped, facing him warily, her posture and expression tense. "What?" she demanded.

Jamie clenched his jaw. "I didn't like the way he looked at you."

She stared at him with those big brown eyes and he felt himself falling, being sucked into them. Into her.

"I didn't like the way he talked to you." He took a step toward her, aware he was on the verge of doing something stupid and not giving a damn. Shit, his breathing was erratic, his heart clattering against his ribs. "I didn't like the way he *touched* you."

Charlie held her ground, unmoving, her eyes searching his, full of stunned disbelief. "Jamie, what...?"

Did she really not understand what she meant to him? His heart hammered against his ribs. "And I don't want you to be alone with him for even one second tomorrow night."

She looked so calm, so composed, and he was about to lose his shit. "I have to be. It's the only way to get to the laptop."

"Fuck the laptop." Even as he snarled it he knew how insane he sounded, how insane he was acting. "Fuck Baker, fuck this entire operation."

"Jamie..."

No.

He stopped directly in front of her, so close she had to tip her head back to look him in the eye, her seductive scent swirling around him. Making him drunk. Or crazy. He had to be crazy to be saying all this. "You asked me why you."

Her eyes searched his, and she nodded.

"You're family oriented. I like that. A lot. I like the loyalty you've shown to your family, and how you helped out Wyatt and your dad when they were recovering. I love that you grabbed a rifle that night in September and ran outside to protect your family and home without flinching—even though it drove me fucking crazy at the same time. I love how brave you were after you shot a man and tried not to show how rattled you were. I admire you for stepping up and taking on this op, even though you're scared, and you should be."

Charlie merely stared back at him, as if at a loss for words.

So he just kept going, the words pouring out of him now. "You know what a job like mine entails, you understand the risks involved and you can handle it. Most women can't. You're independent, which is good, because it would never work between us otherwise, since I'm gone a lot."

Her eyebrows pulled together. "But I'm not—"

"Quiet." He didn't want to hear it. Didn't want to hear why she only wanted a no-strings fling with him. He couldn't stand it.

And he couldn't stand the temptation she posed for another damn second.

He threaded his hands into her hair, a mix of lust and something dark and possessive roaring through him as he stared down into her upturned face. Wide, dark eyes and full, soft lips.

He swept his thumbs across her cheeks, fighting the innate need to take, mark. Possess. She'd broken his control without even trying, and in that moment he didn't care. All he wanted was her.

"When we go there tomorrow night, I want you to remember that you're *mine*," he rasped out, not giving a shit that he sounded like a crazy person. "And I don't want him or anyone else putting their fucking hands on you."

Desire flared in her eyes, and her quick intake of breath shredded the last of his control. Without warning he brought his mouth down on hers and gripped her jaw, the kiss punishing and wild. There was no finesse, no seduction. Just raw need and desperation.

Charlie let out a soft moan and gripped his shoulders, melting into his hold as he plunged his tongue between her lips. The feel of her pliant body pressed to his set him on fire. He didn't even realize he was moving them forward until her back came up against the wall.

Cradling her head in his hands, he leaned his weight into her, plastering them together from chest to thigh. He was so damn hungry for her, wanted to peel that distracting dress over her head, strip off whatever she had on underneath it and devour her mouthful by mouthful until she knew they were meant to be together. That she was his.

Charlie dug her fingers into his shoulders and wrapped one leg around his, rubbing her pelvis against the rigid length of his erection. Jamie groaned into her mouth and pinned her to the wall with his weight, the way she shuddered in his grip making every muscle in his body go taut.

God, he hurt. Would have given anything to rip his pants open and slide deep inside her warmth just to make the ache go away. She was the only woman who could ease his suffering.

"Jamie," she whispered shakily, nipping at his lower lip.

He growled low in his throat and held her there against the wall as he slid his tongue along hers, imprinting the taste and feel of her into his brain. His hands locked in her hair, fisting tight to hold her still and tip her head to the side, allowing him to blaze a trail of kisses across her jaw to the side of her neck.

Charlie whimpered and arched in his arms, pushing him. Testing his strength. It set a match to his already smoldering dominant side.

He held her exactly where he wanted her, not allowing her to move as he nipped, kissed and licked his way down her neck, drinking in her scent and the tiny little moans that slipped from her lips.

But it wasn't enough. He wanted her incoherent. Begging. For her to come for him while he watched. For her to remember this moment forever, remember what he could do to her body.

With impatient hands, he tugged the neckline of the dress aside and down, exposing the black satin bra she wore underneath. For a moment, he stared at the cleavage revealed by the satin cups, then buried his face there, rubbing his hot face against her soft flesh.

She whispered something and squirmed in his hold but he held her in place with his body and pulled the cups of the bra down. Taut pink nipples met his starved gaze, her round breasts heaving with each ragged breath.

On a silent groan, he leaned down to take one succulent peak into his mouth. Charlie cried out and gripped his head now, her fingers digging into his scalp. Jamie cupped her breast and clamped his free hand on her waist, licking and sucking at the tender morsel. She was so soft, so sweet, her body responding to his every caress, her moans echoing in his head.

"Yes." She rocked her hips against him and clutched his head to her chest as he switched to the other breast, following the silent cues she was giving him to give her all the pleasure he could.

Still it wasn't enough. Wouldn't be enough until he made her shatter right in front of him while he watched and savored the triumph of her surrender.

He straightened, captured her mouth once more, now grasping her hips in a firm hold. She met every stroke of his tongue eagerly, rocking into him.

Squeezing one rounded hip tight, he eased his lower body away to give him enough room to slide his free hand down to her left knee. His fingers stroked over smooth, bare skin, warm satin that quivered under his touch.

Charlie made a humming sound and sucked at his tongue, widening her stance for him. He smoothed his fingertips up the inside of her thigh, slowing the kiss now, teasing her while he grazed his fingertips over the baby-fine skin high up on her inner thigh, just inches from the material that covered her core.

When he lifted his head a minute later she stared back at him with dilated, heavy-lidded eyes. Her breaths were uneven, those lush lips parted and a little swollen. So damn tempting he couldn't stop himself from leaning in to suck at the lower one, tenderly flick his tongue over it just as he stroked the pads of his fingers over the front of her panties.

Charlie gasped and trembled, her teeth sinking into her lower lip. "More," she whispered. "I need more."

"You'll get what I give you," he said in a low voice, not even trying to hide the need for dominance that drove him.

He shouldn't have touched her at all. Should have let her lock him out and continue on to his own apartment. He shouldn't have kissed her and sure as hell shouldn't have taken things this far, but he didn't care now. It was too late for regrets, and all that mattered was making her crave what he could give her, something to last them both through the hellish hours until tomorrow's op was done.

Something to make her come back for more when it was all over. To show her he was the one.

He positioned his feet on either side of hers and pushed inward, essentially trapping her thighs together. In their position it was a tight fit but he had just enough room to twist his wrist and slide his hand down the front of her panties to cup her mound. The instant he did his fingers met soft, slick heat.

The breath locked in his lungs.

He stopped, just holding her, letting the heat of his hand and the promise of the friction she needed, build. Her eyes squeezed shut, her mouth opening on a soft cry of need that twisted his insides, her hips pushing into his hand.

"Shh," he whispered, capturing her lips in a slow, seductive kiss.

She parted for him like silk, her tongue twining with his as liquid warmth bathed his fingertips where he stroked between her thighs. Then he pressed the heel of his hand against the top of her mound, putting slight pressure on her hidden clit.

She gasped into his mouth and stiffened, his lips muffling her broken moan. He could feel her thigh muscles tremble as he held her that way, the firm hand on her hip keeping her still for him.

Jamie lifted his head, the blood roaring in his ears and his cock aching as he drank in the sight of her like that. Cheeks flushed, eyes glazed, lips parted and her fingers digging into his shoulders. So damn sexy, even better than he'd imagined—and he'd imagined it plenty over the past year. "Do you know what I want to do to you?"

Her eyes were glazed with pleasure and desire as she focused on him. She shook her head once. Hot. Willing. His for the taking, at least in this moment.

"I want to carry you into that bedroom right now, and lay you down on your back. I want to strip this dress off you and tie your wrists to the headboard." Real restraints. Bands of soft, supple leather that would hug her slender wrists in an unbreakable grip, and maybe her ankles as well.

Molten heat blazed in her eyes, but no shock. She'd already figured out that he liked to take control in bed, didn't seem surprised by him wanting to tie her up. "And then what?" she whispered.

The almost breathless anticipation in her voice sent a shudder snaking through him. "I don't want you to be able to move while I drive you out of your fucking mind," he murmured, shifting his hand slightly, sucking at her lower lip as she gasped and tensed. "I want to find every secret hot spot on your body and use my hands on it…then my mouth."

He slid his tongue over that full lower lip, nibbled at the corner of it. "I want to find out what it takes to make you beg me to let you come, and then I want to keep making you come until you beg me to stop. I want to make you *mine*." His voice was low, guttural, sounding more animal than man.

A soft whimper was her only reply.

The need on her face only ramped his hunger higher. He fought it back, struggled to get his breathing under control as he waited. Waited...

Then Charlie let out a shuddering breath and went lax in his hold, her entire body relaxing.

Gifting him with her trust. Her surrender.

A wild, primal thrill exploded inside him, followed by a tenderness he'd never experienced before. He'd give his life to protect this woman. His woman.

Slowly, lovingly, he rubbed his hand against her core, reveling in the silken feel of her and her sensual response to his touch. She was gorgeous in her arousal, totally uninhibited and comfortable with her sexuality, as he'd known she would be.

She let him watch her, stayed still and held his gaze while he drew his fingertips up her damp folds to delicately circle her swollen clit.

Her eyes drifted shut, her head tipping back against the wall, her expression one of pure, erotic bliss that seared into his brain. "Oh, Jamie, yeah..."

Again and again he circled that fragile bud, part of him wanting to draw this out and make it last, while another part wanted to push her over the edge immediately to show her the mastery he had over her body. She was warm, wet and willing, rocking her hips against his hand in a silent plea for more.

He needed to make her understand that this wasn't a game for him. That he was still playing for keeps. That after tonight, he wasn't letting her walk away.

Charlie made an impatient sound, her submissive posture dissolving as he teased her. Curling a hand around the back of his neck, she gasped and dragged his mouth back to hers.

"You're mine," he muttered against her lips, sliding his tongue into her mouth at the same time as he shifted his hand and slowly eased a finger into her core.

Her fingers clenched tight at his nape, a broken moan escaping her. She was panting now, her entire body quivering, desperate for the release he could give her.

Yeah, pequeña. *All mine.*

He pushed a second finger into her, stroked along the back of her pubic bone with firm pressure while he caressed her clit with his thumb in slow circles.

Charlie broke the kiss, the back of her head hitting the wall with a soft thud, her sensuous whimper like the lash of a whip to his over-stimulated senses. "I'm so close," she gasped out, the hand at his nape pushing his head down while she arched her back, pushing her bare breasts out. "Please."

A growl of triumph locked in his throat. He'd bet he could make her beg so sweetly for him. But right now he needed to earn her trust by giving her the release she needed.

Heart thudding, breathing hard, he dipped his head to take a straining nipple into his mouth and sucked, his hand still sliding slow and steady between her trembling thighs.

Her broken cry of pleasure stroked over his skin like a caress.

He swirled his tongue over the tender peak, thought for a moment about dropping to his knees and replacing the thumb on her clit with his tongue but she was already tightening around his fingers, her inner muscles rippling as she neared the edge.

Jamie ignored her whimpers, the desperate grip of

her hands. He held her hip steady and kept doing exactly what he was doing, refusing to be rushed.

Her breathing grew more erratic, incoherent little sounds coming out of her, then she let out a choked sound and began to come. Her stark cries of pleasure rang unchecked throughout the room, her entire body undulating with each movement of his hand.

Closing his eyes, savoring the moment, Jamie released her nipple and pressed his forehead to the softness of her breast. He stopped the hand between her legs only when she collapsed back against the wall.

Reluctantly easing his fingers from her warmth, he gently cupped her again with his palm, and stayed like that. Soothing her, giving her time to come back down from the high.

When she sighed and stroked her fingers through his hair he straightened and pressed his weight against her to help hold her up, shifting the hand on her hip up to cradle the side of her face.

Those liquid brown eyes were hazy as she blinked slowly at him, her cheeks flushed, hair mussed. She looked like a woman who'd been thoroughly pleasured, and damned if he could summon up even an ounce of regret. "Oh my God," she mumbled.

For the life of him he couldn't come up with a coherent response. His cock throbbed like a toothache against his fly where it pressed against the softness of her abdomen.

Unable to resist leaning in for another taste, he gently covered her lips with his, stroked his tongue between them for an instant before sucking at the lower one, then the upper. She moaned and sagged in his hold, her hand dropping from his nape to his shoulder, her entire body pliant.

He pulled his hand from her panties and slid his arms around her, drawing her into his body so he could hold her close. Charlie went willingly, snuggled into him with a contented sigh that made his heart squeeze. She wound one arm around his neck and slid her free hand down his chest, down to his tense stomach.

Jamie grabbed her wrist before she could reach his waistband.

Her eyes flashed up to his, full of confusion. "You're so hard. I want to return the favor," she whispered, leaning in for another slow, sensual kiss.

Biting back a growl, he nipped at her lower lip and pulled her hand away. "No."

She blinked in surprise, her eyes clearing, then frowned and pushed at his chest to put a few inches of space between them. "No? Are you serious?"

God, he would fucking kill to feel her soft hands stroking over him right now. Or better yet, strip that dress off, sink to the carpet in nothing but her underwear and those heels, then unzip his pants and take him out, close those perfect lips around his cock.

His entire body clenched at the image, a tiny shudder ripping through him.

Except she still hadn't committed to anything more than a fling. And he wouldn't take her without one. Once she was ready for something serious, they could cross that line.

Instead of answering he just kissed her again, already hooked on her taste, addicted to pulling those sweet sounds from her as he made her come. Next time she would come against his tongue and around his cock.

He smothered her protests with a hot, slow kiss, waited until she melted for him again before ending it. His entire body ached with the need to lay her down and plunge into her but that was the worst thing he could do.

Not until she'd agreed to be his. If he gave in now in a moment of weakness, he'd lose her. And that was a risk he simply wasn't willing to take.

Cupping her face between his hands, he swept his thumb over her soft, swollen mouth. "Sleep tight, Trouble," he murmured, catching the flare of shock and vulnerability in her eyes in the split second before he turned away and walked out, back to his empty apartment where a cold shower and a long, lonely night awaited him.

Chapter Nine

C harlie knew she'd found the right dress when she stepped out of the fitting room and Taylor's eyes went big and wide behind the lenses of her glasses.

"Well?" The stretchy black lace cocktail dress had long sleeves and stopped at mid-thigh. Elegant. Classy. And it hugged every single inch of her body.

It also cost three times as much as any dress she'd ever bought before.

"Oh my God, you have to get that one," her friend said in her Texas drawl. Just a year older than Charlie, she'd been transferred to the same office nine months ago as part of the Intelligence Division, in the Organized Crime and Drug Enforcement Taskforce. She glanced around, checking to make sure they were still alone in the room, then adjusted her glasses and lowered her voice to a whisper. "Jamie's going to forget how to talk when he sees you."

"No he won't," Charlie scoffed, even though she hoped he would.

It still stung that he'd walked away last night. He

hadn't left her hanging per se, but now the power balance had shifted between them, and not in her favor. No matter how hard she tried, she couldn't stop thinking about it. About him. What he'd done to her—

No, the *way* he'd done it, all commanding and forceful...

A rush of heat swept through her as she remembered the strength of his grip, his utter sensuality as he'd held her still and taken her apart right there against the wall. And then walked away.

He seemed to do that a lot where she was concerned. She'd had about enough of it, too.

At the time she'd been dumbfounded. In the cold light of day, however, she could understand why he'd left. When he'd told her he played for keeps, he hadn't been kidding.

After he'd pushed his way into her apartment and started kissing her last night, she'd mistakenly thought he'd finally relaxed his stance on the issue. Wrong.

What are you so afraid of? She'd been thinking a lot about that too.

She cared about him. No, more than that. She was falling for him. It complicated things, made her question whether a fling would satisfy her now. And dammit, even though she didn't feel quite as dead set on keeping things casual with him at this point, she bristled at his attitude, the whole my way or the highway thing.

"He will," Taylor argued with a sly smile. "And it's gonna be awesome. I kinda wish I could be there to see his expression."

"I'll take a picture for you," she joked. Taylor knew she and Jamie were attracted to each other, knew what had happened back in April and in September, but didn't know anything about last night.

Though Charlie was dying to talk to her about it, it just felt wrong to say anything. What she'd shared with

Jamie was private, and as far as she was concerned, far from over. That didn't mean she was ready to concede the field and commit to something long term, however.

Once this op was over, she wanted to talk about their relationship moving forward—assuming they would even have one. If he wanted long term as in getting married and having a family, though, they had a problem. She wasn't ready for any of that. Might never be ready for it.

Standing in front of the long cheval mirror, Charlie turned this way and that, looking at her reflection from different angles. The dress was gorgeous and she was sorely tempted to buy it, even if it was obscenely expensive, but...

"Don't you dare put this one back," Taylor warned her. "Who cares what it costs? It's not really your money anyway, so might as well go for it."

True. There was some kind of poetic justice to splurging on something extravagant for herself on Baker's dime, since the DEA was letting her use the money he'd paid her yesterday. "I really like it."

"Well yeah, look at it on you." Taylor snorted and shook her head. "I'd kill for curves like those."

Charlie grinned at her. "This is why I brought you along. You're good for my ego."

"Sure, and that's the *only* reason you asked me to come." Her eyes brimmed with laughter.

Well, there was the added bonus that if any of Baker's people were watching her, this whole scenario fit. What was suspicious about two girlfriends shopping together on a Saturday morning, especially when Baker was aware that she needed to buy a dress?

Taylor—who was running under a fake identity for this op as well—hadn't noticed anyone tailing them though, but it was impossible to know for sure given how crowded Manhattan was. "Okay, sold. I'm getting it."

"Yay!" Taylor stood and hitched the strap of her

purse up higher on her shoulder. "Now we need shoes, then lunch, in that order. Let's go. We're on a tight timeline here." She gestured impatiently for Charlie to scurry back into the fitting room.

Killer cocktail dress acquired, they strolled down the busy street lined with high-end shops in search of shoes. Charlie decided on a bright purple pair with crystals along the open toes, and then they went to find someplace to eat.

"So you never said, but how did your dinner date go last night?" she asked Taylor when they were seated at a booth in the upscale restaurant they'd chosen for lunch. Again, paid for by Baker, which would make the food even more delicious.

Taylor made a face and picked up her menu. "You owe me. That's all I'm gonna say."

Charlie bit back a grin. She was glad to be able to spend some time with Taylor this way. It helped quell the worst of her nerves and took her mind off tonight and what could happen with Baker, which she didn't want to think about any more. "Didn't go well? No second date?" she teased.

"No. Even if he was my type—and he's not even remotely in the right ballpark of my type—I'm not his either. Pretty sure he thought I was a complete, awkward dork by the time we got out of there."

Oh. "Awkward?"

Taylor met her gaze from over top of the menu and shot her a sardonic, heavy-lidded look. "Like you wouldn't believe."

Charlie winced. Her introverted and highly private friend hardly ever went on dates, so being forced to go out with one of Jamie's teammates last minute yesterday to watch her and Jamie's back must have been uncomfortable for her.

Though Charlie had met Logan a few times since the initial team meeting at the start of this op, and liked him.

He was the newest member of FAST Bravo and had a sarcastic sense of humor that Charlie got a kick out of.

"Sorry," she murmured.

Taylor shrugged and went back to perusing her menu. "It's okay, couldn't be helped."

Her friend had never confided in her about her past, but given how rarely Taylor ever dated, Charlie had a gut feeling that something bad had happened to her. Although Taylor was quiet, she was friendly enough, except around men she didn't know. Then she was stiff and clammed right up. Maybe in time she'd feel comfortable enough to tell Charlie what had happened.

"If it's any consolation, my dinner didn't go so well either. It was so uncomfortable, the way the guy kept ignoring Jamie," she said, feeling comfortable talking about this because the restaurant was so noisy.

Taylor set down the menu and regarded her with worried hazel-brown eyes. "He's so slimy underneath that slick image he portrays. And the worst part is, he's the kind of guy who doesn't show his other side until it's too late."

Exactly. Another reason why Charlie was so worked up about tonight.

"Are you... Do you want to talk about tonight?" Taylor offered.

"Nope. Not even a little. I just want to eat and enjoy some girl talk and forget about everything else for a while."

A soft smile curved Taylor's mouth. "Okay." Reaching across the table, she set her hand over Charlie's, squeezed. "It's going to be fine. Jamie and the rest of us would never let anything happen to you."

"I know." Pulling her hand free, she cleared her throat and flagged down their waitress. "Let's get some food."

The rest of the lunch was highly enjoyable. By the

time the bill came, Charlie had nearly forgotten what she had to do in another few hours.

All too soon they were on the subway heading back to Brooklyn. At Charlie's stop she hugged Taylor goodbye and walked the two blocks back to her apartment building.

It was just after two in the afternoon now, leaving her just enough time to shower and get ready before she and Jamie left. He was renting a car for them to make the two-hour drive out to The Hamptons and back.

She tried everything to clear her mind while she stood under the shower, letting the hot water pound down on her head and shoulders in an attempt to ease the stiffness in her muscles. It was easy enough to push thoughts of Baker out of her head when she concentrated hard enough.

But it was impossible to do the same with Jamie. He wasn't the sort of man a woman could ignore, much less forget, and having experienced firsthand a taste of what he offered...

She wanted more. So much more. But exactly how much she was willing to offer in return, she wasn't sure, except it was more than it had been a week ago.

"One more night," she murmured to herself.

All she needed to do was somehow get Baker to turn on his laptop in front of her for a few minutes, and the transmitter would do the rest. Then she could end this charade, get back to D.C. and on with the rest of her life.

How she was going to make that happen, however, was anyone's guess. She and the team had come up with a couple ideas, but until she was in that office with him, she wouldn't know which one—if any—were plausible.

After doing her hair and makeup, she put on a special pair of earrings to complete her look. The cell phone on the bathroom counter dinged with a new text message from Jamie, telling her he'd meet her downstairs in five minutes.

She blew out a long, steadying breath. *Go time.*

Charlie slipped the new encrypted burner phone into a small clutch purse and grabbed the lip-gloss transmitter. Baker's men would confiscate the phone before she went inside the house, but if anyone checked it, they wouldn't find anything incriminating on it.

She'd thought about hiding the transmitter in something else, then decided it was better not to, since Baker was already used to seeing her pull out the lip-gloss. At dinner last night she'd made a point of pulling it out twice, once after dessert and then again before leaving the table. She checked it carefully one last time to make sure the seam in the base didn't show before dropping it into the clutch.

Grabbing the key to her apartment from the bowl on the kitchen counter, she tugged on the hem of her dress and grabbed the shawl she'd bought to wrap around her shoulders if she got cold. Nerves had her pulse skipping as she stepped out into the hallway, part of her still having trouble believing she was actually going to do this.

Jamie was waiting for her downstairs in the building's foyer when the elevator doors opened. Her heart stuttered at the sight of him standing there, tall and mouthwatering in the black tux he must have rented this morning, the width of his shoulders emphasized by the tailored jacket. The crisp white of the dress shirt showed off the gorgeous bronze of his skin, the dark scruff on his jaw giving a rugged edge to his good looks.

His dark-honey eyes locked on her, tracked down the length of her body and back up, and the flash of pure hunger she saw there made her a little weak in the knees. "You look…nice," he said, the hesitation suggesting he'd almost forgotten to stay in character and said something else instead.

Okay, he hadn't lost the ability to talk, but knowing

she'd nearly thrown his concentration was a boost. If Taylor was here, she'd be giving Charlie a supportive thumbs up right now. "Thanks. You—" *Look amazing*— "sure clean up nice."

He grunted in reply, looked like he wanted to say more, but then turned toward the door. "I'm parked in the side alley."

She caught his arm to stop him. He half-turned and she got a subtle whiff of his cologne as she stepped up to him and stopped, her high heels putting her nearly at eye level with him. Standing in front of the front door they were in plain view of anyone who cared to watch them from the street, maybe even people from their team— including her brother—but she didn't care.

This was it. Once they left here, she would be in some degree of danger. They both would. And before that happened, she wanted him to know how she felt, even if it wasn't in words. He was stealing her heart piece by piece, and there wasn't a damn thing she could to do stop it.

She didn't *want* to stop it.

Before she could change her mind, she put a hand on the side of his face, leaned in and pressed her lips to his. *I care about you, way more than I want to*, she told him without words.

Jamie stiffened but didn't push her away. The kiss was soft and sweet and she pulled away after only a second to stare up at him.

Jamie didn't move, holding her gaze, his expression tormented. She knew he didn't want her to do this. Didn't want to be involved with putting her into danger. But neither of them had a choice.

It was too late to back out now. They had a job to do, and if they did it right, starting tomorrow they could build a case to put Baker away, and maybe even bring down more people within the cartel.

"Guess we'd better get going," she murmured.

He nodded once, jaw tight, eyes unreadable. "Yeah." He opened the door for her.

She stepped out onto the front walkway. The afternoon spring air was warm, the sun shining down on her, but she felt colder inside as she moved away from Jamie.

He walked with her around the side of the building where he'd left the car, hesitated a moment at her side as though he wanted to open her door for her, then walked around to climb in behind the wheel. Because this wasn't a date. They weren't a couple, and James her neighbor wouldn't have opened the door for her.

He pulled out onto the street, nodding once at Logan, who was driving a delivery van parked across the street. Easton and Taylor were in there with him. The team would follow them to within a mile or so from Baker's house, then wait there while she and Jamie carried out the op, just in case.

It didn't ease the sense of foreboding building inside her. Having the team wait "nearby" wasn't exactly a whole lot of comfort should something go wrong. The entire taskforce—hell, the entire investigation—depended on her gaining access to that laptop tonight.

Traffic was steady as they drove east out of the city and headed up Long Island. "Have a good time with Taylor this morning?" he asked, sexy and confident as ever behind the wheel. The man played havoc on her nervous system simply by being near her.

The chance for some light conversation helped ease her nerves a little. "I did. She's great. What did you do today?"

"Rented this monkey suit," he said, gesturing down at himself with one hand.

"Perfect fit."

He glanced at her, his gaze sweeping over her with

such heat and longing it made her toes curl in her new heels. "So is your dress."

At that moment, she wished with everything in her that he would turn around, drive them back to the apartment and take her upstairs. Forget about this whole operation and what she had to do. Finish what he'd started yesterday. Figure out where they would go from there.

Maybe when this is all over.

Something for her to look forward to after the stress of tonight. She'd never been interested in anything more than casual before, but then none of the men she'd dated had been anything like Jamie. Plus she loved that he was close with his family, and that he and Easton were so tight. It spoke volumes about his character.

"Thanks." She shifted in her seat, trying her best to ignore the nervous buzz in her stomach, a hive of angry bees growing more and more agitated with each mile they drew closer to Sagaponack.

They made small talk for a little while, but they were careful not to bring up last night or the status of their relationship, and after about half an hour they ran out of things to chat about and lapsed into silence.

Doubt began to creep in, her mind running through all the things that could go wrong tonight. Little by little, dread and anxiety coiled her muscles tighter and tighter as they neared The Hamptons.

Baker was hoping to sleep with her tonight. No sense avoiding that reality. He was definitely going to try to get her alone in the office, and it was probably her only shot at accessing his laptop. She'd have to wing it, adjust to whatever the situation called for, and, if things got sticky, hope she'd learned enough about self-defense from her dad and brothers and the crash course from Jamie to hold her own and escape Baker's clutches.

Her stomach hurt. Realizing she was holding her breath, she consciously relaxed her muscles and inhaled deeply. But the ache in the pit of her stomach didn't go away.

Jamie glanced over at her as the sign welcoming them to Sagaponack came into view. She stared straight ahead through the windshield, trying every trick she knew to calm herself, afraid to look at him in case it gave her away.

It wasn't working.

Her hands were clasped together in her lap, fingers cold and stiff. Unable to stop thinking about it, her mind raced with dozens of different scenarios she might face tonight, each one more terrible than the last.

Too late now. The tension ebbed higher, building the internal pressure that seemed to be centered in her chest.

She was out of time, had nowhere to go but into the mansion waiting ahead. In just a few minutes she had to be Spider, the cocky and edgy hacker who was going to try to bring down the suspected money launderer for the most dangerous drug cartel on this side of the globe.

Jamie glanced over, took one look at Charlie and bit back a silent curse. God, she was fucking terrified, and they had only minutes to go until they arrived at Baker's place.

Her face was pale, her expression pinched, and her fingers were wound so tightly together in her lap that her knuckles were white.

Damn, sweetheart, don't do this to me now. He was having a hard enough time going through with this himself.

Uncurling the fingers of his right hand from around the wheel, he reached over the console and pried one of her hands loose. Her skin was icy, her fingers and palms damp.

He squeezed but she still didn't look at him, so he wrapped his fingers around hers, brought her hand to his mouth and pressed his lips to it. *Come on, Trouble. Hang in there.*

Finally she glanced over at him, surprise eclipsing the dread in her eyes.

"Everything's gonna be fine," he said, drawing on his best acting skills to make himself sound convincing. God, he hated what they were about to do. What she was going to have to face tonight, and that he might not be right there to protect her.

She already knew the plan and the basic layout of the mansion as well as he did, so he didn't bother repeating it. Get in, mingle with the guests, have Baker introduce Charlie to the Civil War weapons expert.

At some point Baker would take her to his office in the basement, on the pretense of showing her his "collection". It twisted Jamie's guts to think of what would happen after that.

If shit went sideways, she was to get out any way she could, alert him via a beacon and exit the house at the prearranged place. He'd already made it clear to her not to wait if he wasn't there when she showed up. She was to immediately leave the property, slip into the woods bordering the house and make it to the rendezvous point where either he or the backup team would come for her.

He hadn't told her that chances were he wouldn't be there. His job was to protect her, give her enough time to get away with the transmitter if necessary. And he was willing to face whatever consequences he would face in order to make that happen, including put his life on the line.

"Just a few more hours and it'll all be over," he said with another squeeze.

Unless she didn't access the laptop.

Or if something happened to her before then.

With effort he mentally shoved the thoughts from his mind and lowered their joined hands to the console. In silence, he rubbed his thumb over hers, trying to provide some warmth and comfort. There was really nothing more he could say to her that would make this any easier.

But there were a hell of a lot of things he wanted to say.

I love you. I hate that you're doing this, but I'm also so damn proud of you and I'm going to make sure you're okay. Once this is over I'm going to tell you exactly what you mean to me, do whatever it takes to make you mine.

Knowing he was only a matter of hours away from getting the chance to say just that was the only thing that made this situation bearable.

"I've got your back," he said instead.

She flashed him a grateful, albeit nervous smile. "I know. And I'm glad."

He'd stay as close to her as possible until Baker took her into the office, and even then he'd wait somewhere nearby. If she needed him, she was to give a signal via one of her earrings, rigged with an electronic pulse that his cufflinks would pick up.

Trouble was, the earrings could only emit a signal over a short distance. If Baker's office had thick insulation in the walls or there was too much concrete or electrical interference between her and Jamie, he wouldn't get the signal.

And even if he got it, he was unarmed. She'd still have to fight Baker off until either she could escape, or Jamie could break into the office. Since he was unarmed, Jamie would have to use the element of surprise and take the guards out hand-to-hand.

If it came to that and he had to go after the bastard, Jamie might break Baker's neck rather than simply incapacitate him for attempting to assault Charlie.

A protective, territorial rage burned in his gut. Realizing he was gripping her hand too tightly, he forced himself to relax and eased his hold. He had to reassure her, boost her confidence, and fast. "I'll be inside the house with you, and the team's nearby. You've got this, Charlie."

She nodded, the motion jerky. "Yeah."

Behind him, Logan flashed the van's lights and turned left off the road. Jamie didn't signal back.

They were all on their own now.

Up ahead, the road Baker lived on came into view. Charlie pulled her hand from his, smoothed the skirt of that sinful dress down her thighs and drew herself tall in the seat as she pulled in a slow inhalation.

It was like watching an actor on set, getting into character in preparation to film an intense scene. She was so fucking brave in the face of her fear, his heart clenched.

He didn't say anything else as he drove down the quiet, forested road, every house they passed worth over ten million easy. Both of them were too lost in their own thoughts to bother with talking now, preparing for the roles they had to play.

Then the sprawling, creamy-colored Italianate mansion appeared up ahead on the right.

Jamie turned up the driveway and stopped at the gate. After letting the guard check their IDs, he drove up to the house, the wheels bumping slightly over cobblestone driveway that ended in a circle, a fountain bubbling in the center of it. A row of luxury cars was parked out front of the long garage.

Some of Baker's rich friends and business associates were already here, some law abiding, and others not. He'd been tasked with trying to identify any key players who might be here.

Jamie parked at the base of the front steps, barely kept from looking at Charlie again. He stepped out and allowed the valet to get in as another helped Charlie out of the car, her tiny clutch purse in hand. She had her game face firmly in place as she smiled at the man, no hint of nervousness in her expression or posture now.

It was amazing to see. Even more so because she wasn't a trained undercover agent. But God, what he wouldn't give to put her back in the car and drive the hell away from this place.

Then she turned toward him, and Jamie caught a hint of unease in those big brown eyes before the street-smart Spider mask slipped back into place. She raised a cocky eyebrow at him. "Coming?"

Yes, ma'am. And I'm going to be on you like a fucking shadow for as long as I can.

Jamie never took his eyes off her as he followed her toward the two security guards dressed in tuxes flanking the huge front door, every sense on alert.

He just wanted this to be over so he could get her the hell away from Baker once and for all.

Chapter Ten

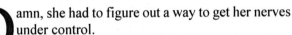

Damn, she had to figure out a way to get her nerves under control.

Charlie paused in the act of scanning the crowded room to snag a flute of champagne from a passing waiter's tray. She didn't plan on drinking the entire thing but she needed something to wet her dry mouth and give her something to do with her hands before she started fidgeting. Broadcasting her nervousness would be a costly mistake.

"Well," she said to Jamie, who stood beside her looking exactly how he was supposed to—bored and like he'd rather be anywhere else but here. "Should we go make an attempt to look sociable?"

He grunted in response but followed her as she made her way across the polished marble floor toward the open archways at the end of the atrium.

Man, she felt like she was in another world here.

The large, spacious atrium was built off the kitchen and led out onto the huge patio that surrounded the gleaming turquoise pool in the center of the back courtyard. Everywhere she looked, men and women dressed in black tie attire stood talking amongst themselves while a violinist and harpist played quietly in the corner, the gentle notes drifting on the warm afternoon breeze.

Everyone here had money. How much of it was dirty money? And how many people were here because they either used, or wanted to use Baker to launder it for them?

The heels of her shoes clicked against the tile floor, seemed to echo in her ears despite the murmur of voices around her. Spider would be polite, but cool. She definitely wouldn't go over and start chatting up a stranger just to make conversation.

No, she'd wait on the periphery, watching the crowd. She would wait for Baker to come to her.

Charlie stopped next to one of the atrium's pillars, raising the champagne flute to her lips. Jamie stood to her left, leaning negligently against the pillar, hands in his pockets. He looked annoyed, bored out of his mind, but she knew he was watching everything.

They didn't have to wait long.

Within a minute the crowd before her rippled with movement, then seemed to part. Baker appeared in the center of the opening, dressed in a white tux, his blond hair neatly parted to one side and a red rose tucked into a buttonhole. His gaze locked on her and a slow smile spread across his face, sending an answering shiver up her spine.

She didn't smile or nod at him in acknowledgment, simply stood where she was and waited for him to come to her, using the remaining few seconds to steel herself for what was coming.

"Charlie," he almost purred, taking her free hand and raising it to his lips. "You look absolutely stunning."

An invisible fist clamped around her stomach and squeezed but she managed to force a polite smile even

132

though her face felt stiff. "Thank you."

He flicked a dismissive glance at Jamie. "James. So glad you could come."

Yeah, right.

"Nice place," Jamie said.

Baker glanced around, nodded. "It's a great place to entertain." He turned back to Charlie, offered her his bent arm with a charming smile. "Shall we? The weapons expert is just over there." He nodded toward the other side of the pool.

Here we go. "Sure." She had to stay in character even if she really wanted to punch him in his lying face.

She slipped her arm through his, repressing the involuntary shiver that touching him triggered. Her heart beat faster as he led her to the other side of the patio and introduced her to the weapons expert, a fiftyish man with a Victorian-style beard and sideburns.

"Robert. This is Charlie, the young woman I told you about."

Robert's pale blue eyes glittered with excitement. "Charlie! Of course. So glad to meet you." He held out a hand.

His genuine warmth and enthusiasm melted some of the ice inside her. "Hello." She shook his hand and introduced Jamie.

Robert immediately began asking her about her family history in the Civil War, then more specifically about her ancestor's weapons. She answered everything to the best of her ability, while making sure to be vague enough that he wouldn't be able to take her information and do a search on her real identity.

Through it all Baker stood beside her, so close he was almost touching her, hands clasped behind his back. He appeared to be listening intently to the conversation, but Charlie could feel the weight of his stare on her and knew he was thinking of other, more explicit things.

She was *so* looking forward to taking this asshole down.

"Has Dean showed you his collection yet?" Robert finally asked as the conversation dwindled.

And there it was. She mentally grimaced. "No, not yet."

Robert cast his friend a shocked look. "What? Dean, you must show her."

"I will," Baker replied. "But I think first she needs a fresh glass of champagne." Before she could argue, he'd waved a waiter over, plucked her mostly untouched and now warm champagne from her grasp and handed her a new one.

"Thanks," she murmured, torn between wanting to leave and wanting to go down to his office right now so she could get this over with and end the torturous waiting.

It reminded her of when she'd been waiting for news about Wyatt after he'd been wounded by that IED in Afghanistan, and when her dad had suffered the stroke. The waiting was always the worst part.

Robert dug in the breast pocket of his tux jacket and pulled out his wallet. "Here's my card. If you send me the make, model and serial number of the weapons, I'd be happy to do some research for you. Free of charge, of course," he added with a smile, and Charlie wished with everything in her that he'd been her mark instead of Baker. Robert seemed like a warm, kind man who genuinely wanted to help her.

"Thank you so much." She tucked the card into her clutch, an idea forming. Maybe she didn't have to go downstairs to see the collection with Baker alone. "I'm guessing that means you've seen the collection?"

"Oh yes, many times. I helped him acquire many of his best pieces."

"Do you have a favorite?"

"I do." His eyes twinkled. "And I'm not ashamed to

admit I envy Dean for owning it. The history behind it is fascinating." He grasped Charlie's upper arm gently. "Come on, Dean, let's go show her." He started to lead her toward the house.

"All in good time, Robert," Baker said, stopping him with a hand on the shoulder.

Shit. Charlie froze, glanced at him. Baker was smiling, but there was a hard glint in his eyes as he drew her away from his friend. "I want to introduce her to some of my business contacts first. Charlie's a wizard with computer systems. I promised to drum up some business for her while she was here."

No, really, I'm good. She pasted on another smile, hoped it looked at least a little genuine.

Robert released her and stepped back. "Of course, of course," he said, waving them away. "Just come get me before you take her downstairs. I want to tell her the stories behind the best pieces—it'll mean way more to her that way."

"You bet," Baker replied, but Charlie could tell he didn't mean it and her heart sank.

She risked a glance over at Jamie, who was watching her closely, then went with Baker as he led her around the patio, introducing her to various business associates of his. The chances of Jamie breaking into the office were slim at best, because of the security personnel Baker had around.

She made it through the blur of forced socialization, managed to give intelligent answers when someone asked her a question even though her mind whirled with what was coming next.

And then, the moment she'd been dreading finally arrived.

"So there you go," Baker said to her, draping an arm casually over her shoulders as he led her toward the house. "You should have enough new business to keep you busy for the next while, and word of mouth is always the best form of advertising. Once word gets out about you, you'll have more business than you know what to do with. You're probably going to have to hire staff," he added, steering her over to the bar set up beneath the arched ceiling of the atrium.

"I'm not sure what to think about that," she replied, feeling dazed. If she hadn't known the kind of illegal things Baker was reported to have done, his charming, helpful act would have completely fooled her.

"It's up to you, it's your business," he said, then glanced at her untouched champagne. "And since you haven't touched your champagne, I'll take that and get you a beer before I take you down and show you my collection."

"Oh, no, it's fine—"

He plucked the flute from her hand and wove his way through a group of people to step up to the bar.

The first stirrings of panic assaulted her. She looked over her shoulder at Jamie, who stood a few yards away, looking awkward and uncomfortable as befit his cover. She couldn't help the fear that had to be stamped all over her face.

Their gazes locked, held for an instant, and she caught the flash of worry in his eyes before she looked away. Baker was at the bar. She watched him take a glass from the bartender and make his way back to her with a beer.

"Here you are," he said, handing it to her. "It's the same kind you ordered at dinner last night."

"Thanks." She had no choice but to take it, made herself swallow some even though she was feeling a little queasy already. Looking over at Jamie, she put on a smile. "Ready to go see some weapons?"

He shrugged and opened his mouth to respond but Baker cut him off.

"Oh, I almost forgot. I have a good friend who was in a car accident last month and has suffered lower back pain ever since. I promised him I'd introduce him, see if James could offer some advice on an exercise and rehab plan he can start, along with the physio he's already doing." He smiled at Jamie. "Do you mind?"

"No, not at all," Jamie answered, his tone calm even though he knew as well as she did it meant he wasn't going to be able to follow her now. "Where is he?"

"Just over here. Gordon," he called out. A tall man likely in his sixties looked over, smiled at Baker. "This way," he said to Jamie, again taking Charlie by the arm and escorting her over. Once introductions were made Baker's grip tightened slightly on her arm. "Well if you don't mind, I've promised Charlie a private tour." He turned to leave.

"I'll come with you if you just give me a minute to talk with Gordon," Jamie said.

Charlie stood there, mentally holding her breath.

"You can catch up when you're done," Baker answered, and pulled her away.

Everything in her wanted to dig in her heels and wrench her arm free of his grasp, but she couldn't. Not without making a scene, and not without letting him know how afraid she was of being alone with him. Besides, this entire operation depended on her doing her job, and getting lucky by gaining access to that laptop, even if it was remotely.

With no choice, she followed him through the atrium and into the house. Catering staff scurried about the huge kitchen, preparing more food for the crowd.

Baker walked her straight past it and through a large sitting room where guests stood around chatting while a pianist played a baby grand. Each note scraped over her strained nerve endings like jagged fingernails.

Her stomach clamped tighter and tighter as they

headed for the staircase ahead of them. What was she supposed to do now?

"Watch your step in those heels," Baker said, gallantly firming his grip to assist her.

She might have appreciated the gesture if she hadn't known he was eager to get her alone downstairs so he could put the moves on her.

God. How was she going to handle this? How far was she going to let him go in order to get to the laptop? She'd gone over various scenarios with the team, but the prospect of having to physically fight Baker put her stomach in knots.

Her heart beat an erratic tattoo as they reached the second level and turned to head down the remaining set of stairs. Two security guards were waiting there. They nodded at Baker and let them pass, and the added confirmation that she and Baker wouldn't be disturbed down here made the growing fear threaten to overwhelm her.

"Just down here," Baker said, escorting her down a carpeted hallway and past two more security guards.

The last door on the left loomed ahead of her, a dark portal that marked the point of no return. A wave of dizziness hit her. She faltered, mentally shook herself.

Baker slowed and glanced at her with a frown. "You okay?"

"Yes." *I just want to do this and get out of here.*

"Come on. It'll be worth it, I promise."

His tone wasn't creepy, but the meaning behind the words chilled her insides.

At the door, he punched in a code to the keypad set into the wood-paneled wall, and her heart sank when a cover slid away to reveal the biometric scanner there. Once Baker closed the door, only he and whoever else was input into the security system would be able to get inside.

He placed his palm against the screen, waited a few seconds while the scanner verified his prints, then a soft beep emitted from the unit and the office door unlocked. Baker pushed it open and smiled at her. "After you."

Oh, God...

Steeling herself, she hid her anxiety as best she could and walked in, still feeling a little lightheaded. A large, expensive-looking desk graced the center of the large room.

Baker stepped inside and reached for the doorknob, then stopped. "You look worried."

"I'm uncomfortable."

He cocked his head, his expression showing surprise that she would admit it. "Why? Are you afraid of being alone with me?"

Yes. Spider would call his bluff right here and now, no games, no pretenses for politeness' sake. "Not as long as you leave that door open." She nodded at his hand on the knob.

A slight smile quirked his mouth. "Your directness is so refreshing, Charlie," he said, and released the knob, leaving the door cracked open a few inches. "Better?"

It surprised her that he'd allowed it. "Yes," she said, and raised the beer glass to her lips once again, aware that her hand was unsteady.

Although an open door didn't necessarily mean she was safe. The four guards between them and the next floor were paid to follow his orders. They wouldn't let anyone else down here and might not come running even if she started screaming.

"Where's the collection?" She glanced around the spacious room, unable to see any other doors.

"In a special room I had designed," he answered, and started toward her with purposeful strides.

Her fingers tightened around the cold glass, the breath hitching in her lungs.

But he merely brushed past her and walked straight to the wall opposite the desk. Again he accessed a secret panel, input a code and then scanned his palm.

A door snicked open to her left.

She half-turned toward it, watched in amazement as Baker pushed the heavy wooden panel open and reached inside to flick on a light switch to reveal a large room stacked floor-to-ceiling with museum quality display cases full of antique weapons. "Wow," she said, the sharp bite of fear fading a little, though the wooziness remained.

"I thought you'd like that," he murmured, smiling to himself as he turned away again and crossed to the opposite side of the room this time. "Just one more thing before I show it to you."

Charlie remained where she was, watching his every move. This time he slid aside a section of bookcase to reveal a safe set into the wall. Her pulse thudded in her ears while he turned the dial on the combination lock.

He reached inside and began to pull something out. She tensed, ready to react if he pulled out a weapon and tried to threaten her—

The laptop.

For a moment, she stared at it in disbelief, then even through the fog clouding her brain she realized she could be giving herself away and tore her gaze off it. She stood there as he placed it on his desk, hardly daring to believe what she was seeing.

"Just need to check something real quick," he said, booting it up.

Now what? She'd expected to have to coax him into it somehow. How to play this casually, so as not to arouse his suspicion?

Aware that she was in his peripheral vision, she took another sip of beer. There was no reason not to because she'd watched him get it, had seen that nothing was put in it.

Stepping closer to the desk, she went to sit the glass down. She pretended to hesitate, looking at the clean surface of the desk before opening her clutch and pulling out the shawl she'd tucked inside, used it as a sort of coaster.

From her position she was less than three feet away from the laptop. It should be close enough.

Trying to ignore the way her heart smashed against her ribs with each frantic beat, she took out the lip-gloss and casually slicked it across her mouth even though her lips felt numb at the moment. The fear almost paralyzed her but she pushed through it, activated the hidden button on the case.

When she looked up, her heart seized. Baker was watching her closely. Too closely. She put on a polite half-smile and straightened.

He kept staring. As though waiting for something to happen. Then he glanced down at her clutch lying on the desk.

Her heart nearly pounded its way out of her chest as that shrewd gaze lifted to hers once more. "You're pale," he murmured. "Something wrong?"

The edge to his tone set off every warning bell in her brain.

Don't panic. You can't panic. Think. You have to be smart, think your way through this.

"I don't feel so well," she mumbled, and she wasn't lying.

"No?" he sat there, his posture and expression reminding her of a cat watching a mouse it was about to pounce on.

A chill raced up her back as he reached across the desk for her purse.

She almost bolted for the door. It took all her remaining courage to stand there and face whatever came next.

He looked inside her purse and withdrew the lip-gloss. Turned it this way and that in his fingers. "You tend to use this when you're nervous, I've noticed." That chilling stare rose to hers once more. "What would you possibly have to be nervous about, now that I've left the door open, I wonder?"

Then he shut off the laptop. Not simply closed the case. Powered it off with the touch of a single button.

"Nothing," she lied, then another wave of dizziness hit her. Stronger than the others. She blinked, put a hand on the desk to steady herself.

"Dizzy?" he asked.

Her gaze shot to his. His expression hadn't changed, his tone wasn't overt, but she heard the menace behind the words.

And then her gaze landed on the beer glass and she understood.

He'd drugged her. Fucking drugged her. But how?

She straightened, shot him what she hoped was a cocky smile, refusing to let him know the drug was affecting her. Stupid. She'd been so stupid to accept the beer… "No. Just not used to wearing heels. But I do need to use the bathroom. Where's the closest one?"

The calm mask slipped, as though the sudden change in script had thrown him. She thought his jaw tightened slightly. "Down the hall. I'll take you."

No you won't. "I'm fine. Be right back."

She didn't dare try to retrieve the transmitter. It had either worked or it hadn't, and touching it now was too risky. She had to cut her losses, get the hell away from Baker and find Jamie so he could get them out of here.

As she walked out the the door, she reached her left hand up and squeezed her earring, hoping Jamie was close enough to receive the signal. With whatever drug Baker had given her already circulating through her bloodstream, Jamie was her only hope of getting out of here now.

Chapter Eleven

For a moment, Dean considered going after her, then stopped himself. She'd be almost to the stairs right now and if he went after her a guest might see and wonder what was going on.

She wouldn't get far anyway, not with his men around. And besides, she truly hadn't looked well. Pale, eyes glassy, swallowing as though she felt nauseated.

He forced himself to take a slow, calming breath, his mind whirling, rebelling against the terrible suspicion growing in his gut. The drug he'd had the bartender slip into her beer had been mild. He'd only given her a small dose intended to relax her, lower her inhibitions enough for him to make her compliant since she so obviously hadn't been ready to come to him willingly.

Unfortunately she'd only taken a few sips, not enough to make her helpless, and something about her behavior just now had set off a warning buzz in his brain that was getting louder by the second.

Moving quickly, he turned his laptop back on and reached for the clutch purse on the desk. Maybe he was just being paranoid, but he'd long ago learned not to ignore his instinct.

He really wanted to be wrong about this. Because if he wasn't…

His lips tightened, but he forced away the regret that assaulted him when he thought of what would happen to Charlie if she'd deceived him. He didn't want her to die.

His hand was unsteady as he took out the lip-gloss. His heart rate picked up when he started a fast-forward of the security footage of the last several minutes, taken from the hidden camera across the room. He'd been checking the feed from the hallway when she'd taken it out, to see if James had come down, to gauge how much time he had for the drug to take effect. It was the sole reason he'd taken the laptop out of the safe.

Then he saw what he'd feared and hit pause, dread coiling in his gut as he stared at the image frozen on the screen. He'd been so intent on his plan, so focused on using that sweet, ripe body, he'd missed the expression on her face and the change in her body posture when his back had been to her while he accessed the safe.

Fixated. Far too interested in what he was doing, even with the drug in her system.

He switched his attention back to the lip-gloss, his heart thudding harder. He fiddled with the tube, searching for anything suspicious. It looked ordinary enough.

Anger and suspicion swirled in his brain as he took apart the tube, the sound of his elevated breathing harsh in the quiet room. She'd made a point of putting some on each time he was near a computer. And at his office the other day she'd set it beside her on the desk as she'd worked. What was she using it for? Recording their conversations? For whom?

With a soft grunt, he managed to pull the tube apart. Shock froze him for a moment as the bottom fell off and clattered onto the surface of his desk…

Exposing what looked like an electronic component wrapped up in a simple rubber band.

His heart lurched in a sickening roll. *No.*

Grabbing it, he ripped off the rubber band, a new fear wrapping its ominous tentacles around his chest. She'd duped him. Deceived him this entire time despite that he'd done a background check on her and believed her story while she'd secretly been plotting to steal from him.

His files. She'd been after his files, and he'd been too blind, had dismissed her as nonthreatening. And for her to have a clean background after the amount of digging he'd done, it had to mean she was working for a competitor.

Or a government organization.

Cursing, he reached into his tux pocket for his phone, his pulse racing. Sweat had broken out on his face, between his shoulder blades. He could feel his tux shirt sticking to his skin. He'd only had the laptop on and open for a few moments. She couldn't have gotten much.

"Where's the girl?" he snapped to the security guard on the second floor. Who the fuck was she? Who was she working for, someone from the cartel? The FBI?

"Just passed by us. Said she was sick, and headed for the east powder room."

"Was there a dark-haired man waiting for her?" *Personal trainer, my ass. More like a trained bodyguard.*

"No. She was alone."

"Watch her and don't let her leave," Dean said, cold seeping into his gut.

He'd known from the moment he'd met Spider that there was something special about her. Something he couldn't quite put his finger on. Now he knew what it was.

She was far more than she seemed, had tried to steal from him.

Now he would bring her down.

"Something wrong?" the man asked.

The rage built, burning through the cold disbelief. He

tossed the electrical transmitter onto the floor and slammed the heel of his shoe down on it, grinding it into pieces beneath his foot.

He would soon do the same to her and her "neighbor". "Yes. And here's what we're going to do about it."

****

Jamie tamped down his impatience as he headed for the open doorway of the gym on the second floor with Baker's "friend" behind him, anxious to find Charlie. Out by the pool he'd spotted no less than five people suspected of having ties to the cartel Baker worked for.

"Thanks for showing me those core exercises. I'll start incorporating them into my routine tomorrow," the man said to him.

"No problem. If you'll excuse me, I need to get back to my friend."

"Of course."

He'd wasted the past twelve goddamn minutes going over planks and other core-building exercises because Baker had neatly trapped him into it to get Charlie alone, and he was strung tight with worry over what was happening downstairs in Baker's office.

Neither of his cufflinks had buzzed but that didn't mean Charlie wasn't in danger. She could have tried to signal him and was simply too far away for the signal to carry.

He didn't even hear what the man said to him as he exited the gym and headed straight for the staircase. Two guards dressed in tuxes flanked the opening, their poses casual, hands clasped in front of them, but their gazes locked on him the moment he came into view.

Shit.

"I'm looking for my friend," he told them, ruthlessly

ignoring the leap of adrenaline in his veins. "Charlie Cooper. Brunette. She went down to Mr. Baker's office with him to see his weapons collection."

One of the guards stepped away from the intricately carved newel post and turned to face Jamie, effectively blocking his way. "I'm sorry, sir. No guests beyond this point."

Jamie kept coming. "I'm supposed to meet them. Mr. Baker invited me personally."

The man held up a hand in warning. "Sorry. The lower floor is off-limits."

Keeping his cool, he shook his head, sized the two men up. Both had to be armed. If he could take one of them by surprise, he might be able to—

Footsteps on the marble steps below caught his attention. His gaze landed on another big man headed up the stairs toward them, also wearing a tux. The man locked eyes with Jamie, and his gut clamped tight. This guy was bad news. Jamie's inner radar was screaming.

"You James?" he asked, and the other two guards angled toward him, their expressions alert.

"Yes." His muscles tensed, preparing to fight. There was no way he could take all three out but if Charlie was in danger then he would take on as many men as it took to get to her. "I'm looking for my friend, Ms. Coop—"

"Sir, come with me." The bad-news guard walked straight past the other two, his expression grim. "Mr. Baker asked me to escort you downstairs."

The hell he did.

Three on one, and he was unarmed. He was well trained in close quarters battle, but taking on three trained guys wasn't going to end well. As the chief guard stalked toward him, Jamie knew he was about five seconds away from getting the shit kicked out of him. So he did the only thing he could.

He squeezed the button on his watch to activate the

emergency beacon to the backup team, then lashed out at the closest man, driving his fist into the man's gut at the same time he swept the guy's legs out from under him.

Before the guy had even hit the ground, Jamie was racing for the hallway that led to another staircase at the far end.

He made it thirty feet before a sharp, hot pain bit into his upper back.

Fuuuuck.

A strangled yell locked in his throat as the surge of electrical current tore through him. He hit the floor on his side, muscles locked, his entire body jerking.

Fight, goddamn you. Charlie needs you.

It galvanized him as nothing else could have.

Through the haze of pain and the black spots dancing before his eyes he saw the three guards running at him. He managed to flop to his back, struggled to gain control of his limbs.

Another surge of electricity jolted him. A heavy weight slammed him into the marble floor, knocking the air from his lungs.

A fist smashed into the side of his jaw. He tasted blood.

A raw cry of rage and denial ripped from his throat. Battling with every bit of strength he had left, he twisted and lashed a fist out at the closest target.

He met nothing but air.

Another blow to the face snapped his head back. More blood as pain bloomed in his nose and mouth. A burst of color and light exploded before his eyes, then everything went dark.

****

Charlie fought the waves of dizziness that threatened to send her sprawling onto the polished marble floor and rushed as fast as she could on the stupid heels toward the atrium. She pulled them off and tossed them aside in her haste to get away. Her stomach rolled and clammy sweat beaded her upper lip and forehead.

The front entrance of the house was closest, but heading out that way was too obvious. She needed a crowd to help conceal her movements. The guards she'd passed by a minute ago thought she was still in the second-floor bathroom, but after waiting a few minutes she'd managed to slip out and make it to the rear stairwell to get by them.

Throwing out a hand, she caught the edge of a fluted column to steady herself and kept going, aiming for the exit point she and Jamie had decided on earlier. People stopped talking and eyed her with concern as she moved through the throng of guests.

One put a hand out to stop her, his expression worried. "Are you all right, Miss?"

She ignored him, focused on sucking air in and out of her lungs and getting to the exit she needed, a gate just off the west side of the garden. What the hell had Baker drugged her with? If her symptoms got much worse than this, she didn't know if she could stay upright, let alone make it out of the property without help.

Panic and determination drove her onward. She hadn't seen Jamie on her way out here but she'd signaled him earlier. He would meet her outside the gate and get her out of here, just like they'd planned.

He had to.

A few people milled about the courtyard garden as she burst through the grapevine-laced arbor that separated it from the patio. She disregarded them all, her sole focus making it to the gate.

Her heart thudded a sickening rhythm against her chest wall as she half-jogged, half-stumbled her way over. She must look like she'd had too much to drink, but didn't care, didn't dare ask for help. This place was probably crawling with criminals who were just as twisted as Baker.

Scanning the garden wall, she spotted the labyrinth of precisely-trimmed yews that marked the western edge of the garden about ten yards ahead. She made straight for it, her frightened gaze searching for the gate in the vine-covered, eight-foot-high brick wall that enclosed the space.

Just as she passed by the labyrinth, a low, familiar voice sounded to her right.

"Looking for James?"

Terror rocketed through her. She froze, jerked her head around to face Baker. There was no one else around to see them.

He stood not twenty feet away, looking every bit the civilized businessman in his white tux, not a hair out of place. But the civilized veneer he liked to show the world ended there.

Now his face reflected the truth of what lay inside. The cold, hard look on his face sent her stomach plummeting to her toes.

He knew.

The spiked beer curdled in her stomach, threatened to come right back up as all the blood drained from her face. She didn't dare speak. What had he done to Jamie?

"You won't find him." The smug edge of a sneer colored his voice.

"W-where is he?" she managed, her tongue thick in her dry mouth, her heart trying to pound its way out of her chest.

"You'll see soon enough."

She'd never save Jamie on her own. She needed to contact the team, get to the rendezvous point.

Run. She took a lunging step toward the brick wall.

Running footsteps crunched over the fine gravel of

the path. Hard, cruel hands grabbed her by the hair a second later, yanked so hard her head snapped back on her neck. She jerked backward, a scream breaking free of her tight throat.

Another hand clamped across her mouth and nose, cutting off her air. Baker. She could taste his cologne, almost threw up.

Twisting, she tried to bite the hard palm, but Baker wrenched her backward and dragged her into the seclusion of the thick yews. A burst of terror detonated in her veins. No. She couldn't let him take her.

"Take her inside." He released her with a shove at his men, the muscles in his jaw working, brown eyes flashing with fury.

She fell to one knee, then his men dragged her backward and lifted her off her feet, one of them pinning her so tightly to his chest that she couldn't breathe.

"Scream and you'll regret it," he warned.

He tugged sharply at the hem of his jacket once to straighten it, and that eerie, calm mask he usually wore slipped back into place. The cold stare burned through her, filling her with ice as the men dragged her away. "You'll excuse me while I go attend to the rest of my guests. I still have hosting duties to take care of before I deal with you." His upper lip lifted in a cold sneer. "Oh, and a word of advice before you leave." He paused, that coldly livid gaze sending a shudder through her aching body. "It'll go much easier on you if you tell them what they want to know immediately, rather than making them work for it."

With those dreaded words echoing in her ringing ears, the goons whisked her across the labyrinth and through a door on the west end of the house, away from prying eyes. Charlie continued to twist and struggle but it was no use. She was no match for the strength of the men carrying her, even without the drug circulating through her system.

She was being swept out to sea on a powerful rip current, being sucked farther and farther away from land, and she was powerless to escape it.

Chapter Twelve

In the passenger seat of the cube van they were waiting in, he let out a jaw-cracking yawn and rubbed at his watering eyes.

"We keeping you up, rookie?" Easton asked from next to him behind the wheel, not bothering to look up as he texted with someone. Probably Piper. Apparently she was going full throttle with all the wedding plans.

"Nah, I'm good." Just bored as hell. It was just like back in his undercover days during those mind-numbing hours of surveillance. Except normally he was the one pretending to be someone else while trying to infiltrate a gang or drug dealer's circle. This time, he was on the sidelines. He'd volunteered initially to be in Rodriguez's position for this op, since he had the most undercover experience. The taskforce higher-ups had decided on Rodriguez instead because of his connection with Charlie.

Logan stretched his legs out in front of him and reached for the now cold thermos of coffee resting in the cup holder between them. For some reason he hadn't slept well last night. He turned his head to look toward the back. "How you doing there, accounting wizard?"

Taylor stopped inputting numbers into whatever program she had open and looked up at him, her brown eyes sharp behind the lenses of her stylish glasses. "What?"

She was so cute, in an anal-retentive, bookworm kind of way. "I asked how you were doing."

She frowned at him. "Fine. Why?"

"Just making conversation."

She stared at him for another second, eyes full of a combination of suspicion and confusion, as though she couldn't fathom why he would do such a thing. "Oh. Well, I'm good." And then she went straight back to typing, dismissing him completely.

For some reason it stung his ego. He couldn't resist digging a little more, just to see how she'd react. "Find anything interesting yet?"

He swore he heard her sigh before she looked at him again with strained patience. "Not yet, but if you'd let me work without interrupting me, I might—" She froze, her gaze jerking back to the screen of her laptop. "Some files are coming through."

At the excitement in her voice, both Logan and Easton swiveled in their seats to stare at her. "From Charlie?" Logan asked.

"I think so." She leaned over the laptop, scanning whatever was on there for a minute or so, then frowned. "It's stopped."

That wasn't good. "Nothing else coming through?"

She shook her head, eyes still on the screen. "What the hell is…" She trailed off, muttering to herself in a way he'd become accustomed to over the last few days. It was kind of adorable. The woman was sure dedicated to her job. "I can't even read it. It's in some kind of code." Her expression was pure irritation as she pulled out her phone and called someone.

Suddenly Easton straightened and looked down at his phone. "Shit."

Logan snapped his head around to stare at him. "What?"

"Fuck. Rodriguez just activated the emergency beacon." He shoved the phone at Logan with one hand as he started the ignition with the other. "Call Hamilton and alert the taskforce."

He dialed their team leader's number, his heart beating faster, and explained as fast as he could when Hamilton answered.

"Where are you now?" the man demanded, voice tense.

"On our way to the backup rendezvous point." He grabbed the edge of the dashboard to steady himself as Easton whipped the vehicle around in a tight U-turn, tires spraying gravel as they turned off the shoulder and raced north down the quiet road toward the secondary RV point.

"Rodriguez is still at the house?"

Logan checked the tracker on the app. The red dot was blinking at Baker's address. He touched the screen, zoomed in so that the house took up the entire screen. It showed the red dot somewhere on the second floor, then rapidly moving toward the east end of the house. "Affirmative."

"How long do they have before you move to the next location?"

The place they would use as a last resort to recover Charlie and Rodriguez before launching a rescue op with police and feds. "Twenty minutes."

"I'll alert the taskforce and locals to be on standby."

If they had to move to a tactical situation, shit was going to get critical. "Roger that." Logan ended the call and watched the beacon on the app. On screen, the dot moved a few yards east, then stopped. And when it started moving again a minute later, it wasn't toward an exit at all. "Looks like he's going down to the basement." Where Baker's office was located.

"Shit, is he going after Charlie?" Easton said as he sped down the road.

"Don't know." But Logan had a sick feeling that neither Jamie nor Charlie were going to show up at the secondary rendezvous point.

****

You're not dead yet. Don't give up. It's not the end. You have to think of something.

It couldn't be the end.

The words kept racing through Charlie's brain on an endless, terrified loop as the two men whisked her down to the lower level, away from any guest and prying eyes.

One of the men carrying her still had a hand clamped over her nose and mouth, presumably to keep her quiet and not draw any unwanted attention to what was happening. Squashed between the two behemoths with her arms wrenched behind her back, she was too exhausted to fight anymore, her muscles trembling and weak yet her body stiff.

She had to be smart, play this right. Baker might be suspicious of her actions but he didn't know who she worked for and likely still thought she was a helpless, clueless civilian. If she was going to mount a final, desperate attempt at escape, she had to conserve her energy. Maybe fool her two captors into thinking she was cowed.

All contingency plans were used up now. If Jamie had truly been captured as well, then they were in deep shit. He was supposed to have alerted the team via a signal from his watch if an emergency situation arose.

The team would move to the alternate rendezvous point, wait twenty minutes. If they didn't show, a tactical assault would be launched to try and rescue them.

She was starting to fear she wouldn't live long enough for it to happen.

It was dark down here, the hallway lit only by dim sconces on the walls. The men carried her through a heavy door at the far end. It swung closed behind them with an ominous clang that echoed off the concrete walls and floor. Her heart smashed so hard against her ribs she feared it might burst.

Without a word they took her to what looked like a steel door and set her down. Her bare feet met the ice-cold floor and she sucked in her first big gulp of air when the heavy hand over her mouth and nose released her. She gasped and wobbled on her feet, didn't have time to draw a breath to scream before one of them pounded a fist on the door.

It opened a few inches, enough to reveal the face of another man, his features harsh and blunt. "What'd he say?" he asked the goons.

"Told her to fess up so you'd go easier on her," one of them said.

"Did he?" The man's pale gray eyes landed on her, the almost gleeful light in them turning her stomach over. "Well for her sake, I hope she takes that advice. I'm not used to working over ladies. Especially not such pretty ones."

His expression and the faint curl to his lips suggested that he was looking forward to the opportunity. Charlie refused to react.

"You can go," he told the others with a dismissive jerk of his chin, and started to pull the door open wider.

Raw terror squeezed her throat shut, flooding her body with a surge of adrenaline. Every sense sharpened. Was he going to beat her? Torture her? She'd never been good at lying, and now with her life at stake, she didn't think she could pull it off. If she told him she worked for the DEA, would it save her, at least for now? Or make things worse?

One of the men holding her released her wrists and shoved her forward with a hard blow between her shoulder blades. Stifling a cry, she stumbled and caught herself on the edge of the doorframe a split second before smashing into it.

Before she could straighten, a beefy hand reached out and curled around her nape, the thick fingers squeezing. She braced herself, gathered her strength to fight, and then the man jerked her into the room.

Charlie gasped and threw up both hands behind her neck to grip the cruel fingers digging into her flesh, but the pressure didn't ease up. It clamped down tighter, the bruising force dragging her up onto her bare toes.

Wintry gray eyes stared down at her from beneath heavy black brows, making the room feel twenty degrees colder than it was. "I heard you're a clever little thing. But not clever enough," he mused, then whirled them around to face the center of the room, holding her tight to his front. The hard, unmistakable outline of a gun tucked into his waistband pressed into her lower back.

Turning her head, she sucked in a breath, a blade of anguish twisting between her ribs at the sight before her.

Jamie.

He was tied to a chair, hands bound behind him to the back of it. A strip of duct tape covered his mouth. Judging by the damage on his face, they'd already worked him over pretty bad.

Blood dripped slowly from a cut over his left eye, which was almost swollen shut. His other stared back at her with a mixture of fury…and regret. Another guard stood a few feet behind him against the far wall, casually clasping one wrist in front of his body.

Slowly, Charlie released the cruel hand vised around her nape and allowed her arms to fall to her sides.

"So, Mr. Baker seems to think James is much more than a neighbor to you," the man holding her said in a low voice, the outline of the weapon digging into her lower spine. "If that's true, then that should speed up this whole interrogation process."

As if to emphasize the point, the man standing behind Jamie reached into his pocket. A quiet snick sounded as he raised his hand to reveal the wickedly-sharp switchblade glinting in the ghastly overhead light.

In that moment, everything crystallized for her. These men were going to torture Jamie in front of her to make her talk, and they wouldn't stop until she told them everything they wanted to know.

Once she did, she and Jamie would both die. She knew it with a gut-deep certainty.

From across the room Jamie stared back at her through his one good eye, the anger and apology there clear. There was nothing he could do, and he would accept his fate in the hope that his death would save her. That was just the kind of man he was.

She bit back a shout of denial, rage and helplessness sweeping through her. She refused to let him die.

From out of nowhere, a strange sense of calm came over her. The raw edge of fear faded, replaced by determination. The man holding her prisoner thought she was helpless.

He was wrong. And underestimating her would prove deadly.

There was no time to think the plan through or second-guess herself. Her only weapon was the element of surprise, and she had to use it *now*.

Afraid she might change her mind or hesitate if she waited a second longer, she pivoted, both hands driving downward to snatch the weapon from the man's waistband. Everything seemed to happen in slow motion, each movement separate, almost disjointed in her frozen mind.

Her right hand closed around the grip of the pistol. The man jerked and immediately moved to grab her wrist. His thick fingers curled around her bones.

Too late.

The muzzle of the pistol had cleared his waistband. She pulled the trigger, hitting him right above the belt at point blank range.

Blood spattered over her, warm and sticky. He grunted and stumbled back against the door, eyes wide. One hand flew up to cover the wound, an expression of shock on his face as blood streamed out of his gut.

Before he'd even slumped down, Charlie was already whirling to fire at the other man across the room.

The other guard lunged toward her, the blade held high, ready to strike. She raised the pistol.

A hard kick to the back of the leg by the man she'd shot knocked her over. She lost her balance, slammed into the ground.

Pain shot through her hip and elbow but she rolled to her side. Lifted the weapon and fired at the man against the door. This time the bullet slammed into his chest. He jerked and cried out, falling to the side.

A muffled shout brought her head around.

The man with the knife was mere steps away from her, his body coiling to strike. Yanking her arm to the right, she fired.

The bullet struck him in the upper thigh. He screamed and lurched forward, clutching his leg.

Jamie exploded into motion.

He kicked both legs up and out, using his momentum to jump to his feet. Then he whirled, slamming the back of the chair into the man's shoulder. The knife hit the floor and clattered toward the opposite wall.

Both men hit the concrete floor with a bone-crunching thud. Jamie landed on his back, still trapped in the chair.

As the wounded man fought to get up, Jamie flung his legs out and wrapped them around the man's throat from behind, then twisted. The guard choked and grabbed at Jamie's legs, trying to pry them free, his face red, eyes bulging.

Charlie rolled over and scrambled unsteadily to her feet, advancing on them with the pistol aimed at her new target. But there was no way she could fire without risking hitting Jamie. He was too close to the man as they writhed and twisted there on the floor, and her hands were shaking.

Pass out, she willed the wounded guard. *Pass out, damn you!*

She stood where she was and held the weapon trained on him, her ears perked for the sounds of someone approaching outside in the hallway. The suppressor had muffled the gunshots but there might be hidden cameras in here, so someone might have seen what she'd done. More guards might be on their way here already.

Jamie's face was as red as his victim's as he maintained the pressure with his legs. But the man's struggles were growing weaker, uncoordinated. He flailed a few more times, then his eyes rolled up in his head and he went limp.

Even when he slumped over, apparently unconscious, Jamie didn't relent, maintaining the pressure with his legs for another few seconds before releasing him. He was panting, the labored sound loud in the still room as he raggedly sucked air in through his nose.

Without pause Charlie darted over and grabbed the fallen blade from the floor, then hurried around behind Jamie and started cutting at the plastic restraints around his wrists. "Don't move," she warned, her voice as unsteady as her hands.

The blade was razor sharp, a blessing and a curse

considering how badly she was shaking. Maybe the lash of adrenaline had counteracted the drug in her system, but whatever it was, she didn't feel as woozy anymore. With a few slices she managed to cut Jamie's left hand loose, then the right.

The instant he was free he shoved to his feet and grabbed her wrist, ripping the tape from his mouth with his free hand, his wrists were raw and bloody from where the cuffs had cut into his skin. "We gotta go," he gritted out, his voice harsh in the stillness.

She didn't protest when he took the weapon from her and pulled her toward the door. The man she'd shot was lying sprawled in front of it, blood seeping around him in a shiny crimson pool.

His wintry eyes were still partially open, glassy, staring up at her with what seemed like a mixture of hatred and accusation as he struggled to breathe, the rattling sounds sending chills down her backbone. Charlie swallowed, her stomach pitching, and circled him warily.

"Stay back," Jamie warned her, pushing her away from him as he approached the man. They took a few seconds to look for other weapons, but found nothing besides a cell phone. Jamie yanked the guy by his leg, dragged him a few feet away from the door, then reached a hand toward her without looking back. "Come on."

On rubbery legs Charlie closed the distance between them and grasped that outstretched hand. Jamie's fingers contracted around it, warm, sure.

He paused at the door, head cocked as he listened, gun hand on the knob. Then he glanced at her. "We have to get out of the house, off the grounds and into the forest. We'll use the exit on the northeast side, closest to the water. It's the only chance we've got to make it out of here and get to the secondary rendezvous point."

She nodded, not trusting her voice, suddenly becoming aware of how hard her heart was beating again, and that the soles of her feet were coated with slick warmth. Because she was standing in a puddle of her victim's blood.

She swallowed the bile rising in her throat, ordered herself to hold it together. She'd had no choice but to kill him.

Jamie glanced down at her feet before meeting her gaze once more. "Are you going to be able to run barefoot?"

Another nod, and she clenched her jaw to keep her teeth from chattering. She didn't have a choice, would just have to suck it up and ignore the pain in her feet once they got outside, because it would slow them down too much and draw too much attention if Jamie tried to carry her over his shoulder.

"Okay. Let's do this." He twisted the knob, opened the door a fraction and checked up and down the hallway. Then he pulled the door wider and tugged on her hand.

She swept out into the hall with him, risking a glance behind her. The hallway was empty, but she wasn't sure for how long, and they were leaving bloody footprints with each step.

There had to be security cameras down here. Someone would see them. They might have only seconds to make it out of the house.

Jamie rushed them down the remainder of the hallway, headed for the door that would lead them to the side lawn. There was no cover out there except for a few shrubs, but they couldn't risk trying to find another route now.

Her choppy breaths scraped at her tight lungs as they rushed for the exit. Jamie turned right and then the door was there, directly in front of them at the far end of some kind of mudroom. Hope and relief shot through her veins, giving her an added boost of energy. She could almost smell that salty sea air, all but taste freedom.

Jamie paused beside the door, one hand gripping the knob. She tried to slow her breathing, turned her attention to the doorway behind them. The sound of approaching footsteps down the hall sent a wave of adrenaline shooting through her.

Jamie opened the door, pistol up. Charlie plowed straight into his back as he skidded to a halt with a curse.

Heart careening in her chest, she peered past his shoulder and immediately saw why he'd stopped.

Four armed men stood in a semi-circle not fifteen yards away, weapons trained on them.

Charlie's lungs seized. There was no way Jamie could take out all four of them before they killed him. She stayed frozen behind him, not daring to move, out of ideas, and the rushing footsteps coming from behind them meant there was no escape. Shit, what now?

"Drop the fucking weapon," the man in the lead growled at them, the muzzle of his pistol aimed dead center at Jamie's chest.

Jamie's jaw flexed once, then he slowly lowered the pistol and placed it on the ground.

"Kick it over there," the man commanded, jerking his chin toward the wall to their left.

Jamie complied, the sound of the gun sliding across the tiled floor scraping over her taut nerve endings. He raised his hands, held them there, his body tense but motionless, and she did the same.

The men behind the leader parted. Late afternoon sunlight poured through the open doorway, glinting off a thatch of blond hair.

Baker stepped into view.

His cold gaze swept over Jamie first, then Charlie. An icy, sardonic smile curved his mouth. "That's the second time I've underestimated you, Charlie. But it'll be the last." Pure rage blazed in his eyes as he stared at her. "So now you two are coming on a little private tour with me. Since you're apparently so interested in stealing information about my personal business dealings, I'm going to give you a one-way guided tour of my latest project. And once we get there, we're going to have a little chat."

Chapter Thirteen

I t was deathly silent inside the team van as the seconds ticked by. Even Taylor was quiet in the back now, the absence of clicking on her keyboard adding to the growing sense of tension between the three of them.

Logan glanced at his watch for what felt like the hundredth time. They only had two more minutes until the deadline hit and there was no sign of either Rodriguez or Charlie.

Beside him, Easton made a growling sound deep in his chest and ran a hand through his hair in agitation, his other clamped around the steering wheel. "Is the beacon moving yet?" he asked for the tenth time, leaning over to look at Logan's phone.

"No." That damned red dot that marked the location of Rodriguez's watch had been stationary for the past eighteen minutes. Something was definitely wrong. Either Rodriguez had been taken prisoner, or they'd found out about the beacon somehow and stripped his watch to throw them off the trail.

The phone rang in his hand. His heart jumped, but it

wasn't Rodriguez or Charlie calling. It was Hamilton, who was still back at headquarters in Virginia, and likely looking for an update.

Logan exchanged a look with Easton as he answered, and put it on speaker. "Still no sign of either of them, and the beacon hasn't moved since right after he activated it." They had to stay here until the time was up though, just in case either teammate made a last-second appearance.

Their team leader expelled a harsh sigh. "Well, there's a good reason for that."

Oh shit. "What?"

"The taskforce just got a tip from our lead informant on the case. Apparently Baker just called him, asking him to send Baker's private pilot to a building site on the west end of Long Island. According to the informant, it's Baker's latest pet project, a resort, and the foundation's being poured today. And, he just ordered a bunch of transit mixer trucks to be sent to the site immediately."

Easton's whole face hardened. "You think Baker's taken Rodriguez and Charlie hostage and is transporting them there?"

Or their bodies.

Logan prayed that wasn't the case, but knowing Baker was attached to a cartel known for its viciousness, it was a definite possibility. Christ, what would they do if Charlie and Rodriguez were dead? Easton would lose his shit, and Logan didn't have a clue how to help the guy if the worst happened.

They couldn't go kick down Baker's front door though, so they had to stick to the plan and give Charlie and Jamie a chance to escape on their own first, which was why Logan and the others would head to the secondary rendezvous point.

"Sounds like they're traveling in two or three vehicles," Hamilton said. "The informant mentioned Baker's done something like this before."

"Concrete trucks," Easton repeated, his tone wooden, his face contorted with a mixture of rage and fear.

Hamilton hesitated a moment before answering. "There's no easy way to put this, Easton, so I'm just gonna say it. The informant says Baker's planning to bury them in the foundation."

Taylor gasped in the back.

"Jesus fucking Christ," Easton burst out, shifting in his seat, his body language that of a caged lion. "Did the informant know if they're both still alive?"

"When Baker called him ten minutes ago they were. But the truth is, we just don't know how much time we have left to extract them. Baker could have anywhere between two and six men with him. We're mobilizing the local response team right now."

"If they show up and my sister and Rodriguez are still alive, Baker will kill them for sure," Easton argued. "No way. They need to stand down and let us try first. Granger and I can move to intercept them."

Fuckin'-A. Logan was so down with that plan. The two of them could take the cars by surprise, neutralize most of the armed guards before they realized what was happening. "If we're going, we need to move *now*, sir." But it wasn't his call, or even Easton's. It was Hamilton's. And their team leader risked a shit-ton of serious fallout for letting them off the chain if this didn't turn out in their favor.

"All right. What do you want me to do in the meantime?" Hamilton asked. "You're gonna need backup."

Logan exchanged a long look with Easton. They couldn't track Rodriguez and Charlie via the beacon anymore, but if they knew the end location, they might be able to surprise Baker and get there in time to save Charlie and Rodriguez.

If they were still alive.

"Give us the address of the site, and the name of the concrete company," Easton said.

"Someone's texting it to you all right now. The rest of the boys and I are heading to the airport with a few others to catch a helo up there. For right now, let's come up with a game plan and get moving, because if they're still alive, Rodriguez and Charlie are running out of time."

****

Charlie threw out a leg to keep from crashing into the roof of the trunk as the car hit another bump in the road. Jamie grunted at the impact and tried to angle his body to brace her when she landed.

While she appreciated the effort, it was useless. With limited mobility, no way to talk and being in complete darkness back here, there was nothing he could do for her. By the time they arrived at wherever Baker was taking them, they'd both be battered and bruised.

The tape slapped over their mouths prevented them from speaking, and with their wrists secured behind their backs, they only had their legs for leverage. They'd been traveling for about forty minutes or so, best she could figure.

She kept alternating between a choking fear and a sense of unreality, some part of her brain refusing to accept that this was happening. She thought Jamie had attempted to kick out the tail lights a couple times, but so far it hadn't worked.

Where was Baker taking them? Was the fact they were still alive a sign that there was still hope they might survive this? She had no idea what his plans were, but if he was bothering to transport them somewhere, then it didn't make sense for him to just kill them once they got there.

Did it?

The vehicle slowed and made a right turn. The road was smoother here, with fewer bumps. Charlie wiggled closer to Jamie and pressed up against him. He rolled to his side and curled around her, throwing a leg over hers to anchor her. Wrapped around her like that, he nuzzled the back of her neck with his nose.

For some reason that affectionate gesture brought tears to her eyes.

Things had gone so horrifically wrong. They'd been forced to kill two of Baker's men. Surely he was going to want revenge for that, on top of the way she and Jamie had manipulated him.

It was hard to keep her mind from spinning off to the possible forms of torture and death they were facing. She didn't see any way out of this, didn't know how Easton and the others would ever find them. Baker's goons had taken Jamie's watch off, so they had no way of tracking them. Without a doubt her brother would come after her; she just didn't know if it would be in time.

Squeezing her eyes shut, she focused on the feel of Jamie pressed tight to her back. His warmth and strength. This was probably the last time she'd ever be with him. And if they were going to die today, she prayed it would be quick.

A man like Baker would never let it be quick. Especially not after what you did.

She swallowed, tried to stop the sudden leap of her heart. Then the car slowed again, this time turning left. And then right a few seconds later.

They had to be getting close.

Charlie pulled in a deep breath through her nose and pushed back harder into Jamie. He made a low sound of reassurance in his throat and nuzzled her again.

This time she couldn't stop the hitch in her breath, a sob locking deep in her chest. She didn't want to die, couldn't bear the idea of seeing him tortured or killed in front of her. There were so many damn things she wanted to say to him—wished she'd said to him while she'd had the chance—and couldn't now.

She also thought of her family.

Of her brothers, and her father dealing with her death, knowing she'd been murdered at the hands of a criminal she'd been trying to bring down.

Easton would never forgive himself. It would shatter him. Her poor father…this might literally kill him. He refused to admit how badly the stroke had debilitated him, did everything in his power to make the world think he was still strong and robust, but he wasn't.

God, had it been worth it? Risking her life for this op? She doubted the transmitter had sent more than a handful of files; there just hadn't been time. So if she died, it would be in vain.

Silent, unwanted tears gathered in her eyes. They slipped down her right temple and over the bridge of her nose to drip into her hair, her shoulders jerking under the force of the pressure in her chest. Jamie made another low sound, and even without words she could hear the plea in it.

Don't, pequeña. *Don't cry.*

The car came to a stop and the engine shut off. A rush of icy fear froze her tears, every muscle in her body locking tight. Doors opened, muffled voices sounded nearby. She hurriedly wiped her eyes with her shoulders, not wanting Baker or any of his men to see how terrified she truly was. She refused to give them that satisfaction.

Footsteps came around to the back of the car. A second later the trunk popped open.

She squinted as bright light split the darkness, turning her face away from the glare. Rough hands reached in and dragged her upright. She went rigid, fought to gain her balance and scrambled with her bare feet to gain leverage as the man unceremoniously yanked her out of the trunk and dumped her on her feet. She winced as sharp gravel dug into her tender soles and staggered for a second before widening her stance to regain her balance, and looked around.

They were at some kind of construction site in its early phase. A chain link fence enclosed the area beyond where the two cars were parked. Cranes and other heavy equipment ringed the various squares for the foundation dug into the ground, but nothing was moving and she didn't see anyone on site. The silence was unnerving.

A tall, well-built man in a black T-shirt and cargo pants stepped in front of her, his eyes hidden by dark sunglasses. Another man stood a few feet behind him, observing everything, and two more men dressed like the others were pulling Jamie from the trunk while he twisted and kicked at them, to no avail.

"This one's still got a lot of fight in him, boss," one of them said with a laugh, then slammed his fist straight into Jamie's stomach.

Jamie blanched and doubled over, face pinched as he struggled to suck in air. The men shoved him sideways, sending him sprawling to the gravel on his knees. As soon as he hit, one of them pulled out a pistol and pressed it to Jamie's temple just as Baker came around the back of the trunk.

Charlie's entire ribcage contracted in terror. She couldn't handle seeing Jamie die. Couldn't even bear the thought. She'd beg, do whatever she had to in order to save him.

"That's because he's no ordinary personal trainer," Baker said with a sneer, his gaze shifting to her. "Is he, Charlie?"

She couldn't have answered even if she'd wanted to because of the tape, and she was too afraid to look away from Jamie anyway. Her mind spun, desperately trying to think of a way to save him. Baker would know if she lied. He'd hurt or kill Jamie for sure.

"Pull the tape off her."

The man closest to her stepped up and ripped the duct tape off her face. Charlie winced at the sudden burn, and licked her dry lips.

Baker moved a few paces closer then stopped, arms folded across his chest, still in that immaculate white tux. Behind him, a freshly dug pit yawned in the earth, the large square still empty. "You killed two of my men."

Charlie tensed her thighs to keep them from shaking and didn't answer.

"If any of my personal files transferred to whoever you're working for, it's going to take them some time and effort to decode them—if they ever do. One of the things they'd find is over there," he said, nodding over his shoulder before looking back at her. "That's the start of what's going to be a multi-million dollar resort, which my investors and I are funding. After what you did today, I wanted you to see the progress up close and personal." With that he nodded at his men.

Two of them converged on Charlie. She shrank away, but wasn't stupid enough to try and run. "What are you going to do?" she blurted as the men clamped steely hands around her upper arms and began towing her toward the edge of the pit. At a pained grunt she looked back in time to see Jamie sag in his captors' grips, his good eye squeezed shut, face pinched with pain.

"Bring them over here," Baker said, stalking off the gravel road and toward the edge of the closest pit, past an excavator and front end loader waiting there, along with several concrete trucks lined up in a row, their huge drums turning slowly.

The sharp edges of gravel dug into her bare feet as the men dragged her toward Baker. He walked past the concrete trucks and stood poised on the very edge of the hole in the ground, maybe forty feet long, twenty feet wide and ten feet deep. From what she could see, there was only one way in and out of it, a small dirt ramp just behind Baker.

The men hauling her forward stopped near the edge, and Baker swung around to face her. The arctic fury in his eyes sent a shiver of foreboding through her. "What's your name?"

She couldn't tell him her last name though. He would definitely try to target her family as retribution. "Charlie."

"And him?" he nodded at Jamie.

"Jamie."

"And you're not really neighbors."

She didn't answer, because he already knew the answer to that one.

Baker shook his head, a fake expression of regret on his face. "It's a goddamn shame it's come to this, Charlie. I really liked you."

Yeah, so much you drugged me so you could fuck me and then do God knows what. The bitter words burned inside her but she didn't dare say them aloud.

He cocked his head slightly. "Do you even have an ancestor who fought in the Civil War?"

"Yes." God, why was he playing with her like this? How much should she tell him? Because she'd tell him every last detail about the op if it would save her and Jamie. And she was betting he knew it.

"Bring him here," he said to the men holding Jamie. They jerked him to his feet and dragged him forward.

Charlie's heart lurched as they stopped and spun him around to face her. Staring back at her, Jamie gave a subtle shake of his head, as though trying to warn her not to tell Baker anything more.

Well, tough shit. They were both bound and helpless, and one of the goons had a fucking gun shoved against Jamie's temple.

Baker's voice was calm and clear, the underlying steel in it unmistakable. "You're going to give me answers, Charlie, or your partner will suffer the consequences. My men will start with a bullet in each of his knees, and work their way up. If that doesn't get me what I want from you, the last one will be in his head, and then they'll start on you."

"No, don't," she protested, the words bursting out of her, the pressure in her lungs unbearable. "I'll tell you. But first, let him go."

At that, Baker's eyebrows shot upward. A slow smile lifted one side of his mouth. "Look at you, being all noble even though I can smell from here how fucking terrified you are. But no, not a chance." He signaled at the concrete trucks. The engines fired up and their big drums started turning.

Then Baker nodded at the men holding Jamie.

Jamie kicked and struggled with the hired muscle, until one of them slammed the gun down on the back of his neck. Jamie went limp and the man tossed him backward, down the earthen ramp into the pit.

Charlie let out a shrill scream and lunged forward as Jamie toppled out of sight, heart in her throat. A strong hand grabbed her by the upper arm, fingers squeezing tight as he hauled her backward, pinning her against his solid frame with both arms around her chest.

Baker stared back at her with dispassionate eyes. "He's still alive. Unfortunately. How many holes are you going to allow us to put in him?"

"What do you want?" she gritted out, fury lashing through her. It felt a hell of a lot better than the choking fear. If she'd been free she would have flown at the son of a bitch and attacked him with her bare hands.

"Who are you working for?"

She glared back at him, letting him see the raw hatred and loathing she'd been suppressing these past few days.

Baker's gaze shifted to the man beside him and he gave a slight nod. The goon pointed his weapon into the pit and fired at Jamie.

"No!" Charlie screamed, yanking against the restraining hold around her arms. Jesus, they'd shot him. She didn't know where, didn't know how bad it was. And they'd just keep doing it until Jamie was dead.

She refused to let Jamie suffer more than he already had.

"Who," Baker demanded, the calmness in his voice making him sound a hundred times scarier than if he'd screamed it.

Charlie swallowed convulsively, locked her knees to keep them from shaking even though her entire body was quivering. Lying was pointless now. "The DEA."

His mouth tightened. "The DEA," he repeated, his tone and expression dripping with disgust. "Are you an agent?"

She shook her head, mind spinning like bare feet on a slippery floor. Racing and getting nowhere. She didn't see any option but to keep answering, try to keep him talking, and his attention away from Jamie. "Computer analyst."

"And him?" he nodded toward the pit to indicate Jamie.

There was no way she'd tell him that Jamie was a FAST member. "Agent." She was so scared, didn't know how badly he'd been injured by that bullet, or if he was even conscious. Right now, she was his only hope. *Their* only hope.

Baker's jaw flexed. "Is there even a Spider?"

She nodded, the motion stiff and jerky, her heart clattering against her ribs. Maybe if she could feed him enough truths, it would show she was willing to give him information and it would buy them time. So they could...she didn't know what.

But Easton and the others would know by now that something was wrong. She was sure they'd mount some kind of rescue attempt, since she and Jamie hadn't shown up to the secondary rendezvous point. "Yes, she's real."

"So in order to use her to get to me, it means you must have been working with an informant. Which means one of my own betrayed me." His nostrils flared, that hard stare boring into her. "Who is it?"

Oh no... Her stomach dropped. He'd think she was lying, but she told him the truth anyhow. "I c-can't remember his name." Tom? Tim? "I never had contact with him. Just m-my superiors did."

"Is that right." After a long, taut moment, he squared his shoulders, and something about the change in posture made Charlie's heart stop beating. "Throw her in there with him," he said to the man holding her. "They're going to die together."

"N—" Charlie's legs felt numb as the man bulldozed her toward the edge of the pit. No matter how hard she twisted and fought, she couldn't break free. Couldn't stop what was coming.

Her hair whipped into her face as she thrashed, trying to sink her teeth into the man's arm or hand. She caught a glimpse of the dirt ramp, the smell of it strong in her nose, then was shoved forward.

A terrified scream erupted from her throat as she pitched over the edge and fell into nothingness.

Chapter Fourteen

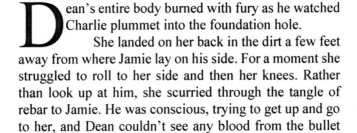

Dean's entire body burned with fury as he watched Charlie plummet into the foundation hole.

She landed on her back in the dirt a few feet away from where Jamie lay on his side. For a moment she struggled to roll to her side and then her knees. Rather than look up at him, she scurried through the tangle of rebar to Jamie. He was conscious, trying to get up and go to her, and Dean couldn't see any blood from the bullet wound.

"Don't bother," Dean muttered to her under his breath, still fuming. Knowing they were going to die didn't ease the rage eating at his insides. Someone from his inner circle had betrayed him. It was the only way the DEA or whoever else could have set this entire thing up.

And the one name that immediately came to mind, was Tim. He was the one who had set up the meeting with "Spider"/Charlie in the first place.

Because Dean had asked him for help.

A whole new level of anger hit him. He'd trusted Tim. With his business, and his life. For years. Had the feds made him an offer he couldn't refuse?

If Tim was behind this, he would die. Slowly, to maximize suffering. Baker didn't like to do the dirty work personally these days, and he knew plenty of people he could hire to make that kind of torture last for weeks, for the right price.

It would be money well spent to spread the message he was not to be fucked with.

Turning toward the first concrete truck, he gave the driver the signal. The chute was already deployed into the foundation hole.

Within seconds, wet concrete began rushing down the chute. It splattered a few yards away from his victims and quickly spread out in a thick gray wave. He pulled in a deep breath and let it out slowly to calm his racing heart, reminding himself to be calm, that it would only be a few minutes more.

The last time he'd done this, he hadn't stayed to watch. This time, he wasn't going anywhere. He wanted to stay while these traitorous motherfuckers flailed and struggled to escape the tide of death slowly coming for them. If they tried to climb out of the hole, he'd have his men shoot them. Dean wanted them both alive when the concrete finally closed over their heads, suffocating them, entombing them forever in the foundation.

And every time he thought of this place, he would remember this moment. His victory, however hollow it might be.

Because the two people he was about to kill had ruined everything.

Even if Charlie had only managed to transfer a small percentage of his files, it was still too much. Any data transferred to the DEA and whatever other agencies were investigating him put him at risk.

His only option now was damage control. As soon as these two assholes were dead, he'd leave the country for a while.

His pilot should be arriving any minute, to take him to a private airfield where a small charter jet was being readied. He'd ride out the storm from the sunny shores of Panama, figure out what kind of damage this would cause him and his business. His clients would want answers. Some of them might want to end doing business with him.

Some might want him dead.

Down in the pit, Charlie and the DEA agent were trying to scramble out of the rebar grid before the wave of concrete reached them. Dean stood there, staring down at them because he didn't want to miss a moment, that hard, searing knot of rage burning a hole in his chest.

He should have fucked her while he'd had the chance. If he'd stopped her from leaving his office, he could have at least enjoyed breaking her before bringing her here.

But this would have to do.

A muted thump from overhead brought his head up. Craning his neck back, he saw the sleek Bell 407 slice through a puffy white cloud, already in its descent.

Right on time.

He turned back to the pit with a grim sense of satisfaction, ready to enjoy the show.

****

Have to get out. Have to save Charlie.

Jamie's entire body felt like one gigantic, pulsing bruise. The bullet had missed and he didn't think he'd broken anything in the fall, but maybe the roar of adrenaline in his veins was muting the pain.

He bit back a groan and struggled to his feet as the tide of concrete continued to rush toward him. He wrenched his head to the side, ignored the sickening stab of pain in his head that threatened to send him back to his knees. The world tilted, went blurry for a second, but he maintained his footing and found Charlie.

She was several yards away struggling to stand, her arms still bound behind her, but no tape across her mouth. Her deep brown eyes met his, wide and terrified. "Can you walk?" she called out.

Unable to answer, he nodded, pushing his way toward her. The concrete was already lapping at his ankles, thick, sucking at his shoes.

He tried to scramble out of the way, but the tight, square pattern of rebar a few inches off the ground hampered his movement. In her haste to get out of the way of the concrete Charlie tripped over one of the pieces and went down hard on her side.

No.

Jamie lunged toward her, determined to get her up so they could escape the rapid flow of concrete. Somehow he had to get her to follow him and run to the opposite side of the pit.

And then he'd have to come up with a way to climb out while their hands were bound and shooters stood less than thirty feet away, waiting to pick them off.

Out of the corner of his eye, Jamie saw Baker wave at the second truck. More concrete poured into the pit, doubling the rate of flow.

Baker and his men were still up there on the edge. They would shoot at some point, but he and Charlie had no other choice but to run now. Escaping the concrete was the first priority. With how fast it was flowing in, staying put meant certain death, and he was still praying for a miracle in terms of some kind of backup arriving. If Easton and the others had received the signal from Jamie's watch, they'd be working to find them right now.

He was almost to Charlie now. Her face was a mask of panic when he reached her. He bent to give her the support of his body along her side as she found her footing. Over the noise of the concrete trucks, he heard the sound of more engines. Glancing up, he spotted two more mixer trucks pulling up to the edge of the pit between Baker and the other trucks.

"He's gonna bury us alive," Charlie cried, wobbling as the concrete crept higher and higher up their calves. She took a slogging step, tripped on another piece of rebar and knocked him over. They both fell, the thick gray sludge engulfing them, dragging them downward.

Jamie heaved upward, his heart wrenching as Charlie rolled to her knees, most of her body covered in gray concrete. Fuck, he wished he could talk.

"The only way out is where Baker is standing," she said, concrete-coated hair sticking to her face and chest, the despair in her voice killing him. "What are we going to do?"

Jamie stopped and glanced back at the bastard responsible. Baker hadn't given his men the order to fire again, apparently satisfied by being able to watch him and Charlie flail around down here until the tide of concrete overwhelmed them.

For now, anyway.

The earthen ramp stood only a half-dozen yards away, but it might as well have been a half-dozen miles. There was no way they'd get to it before Baker's men shot them down, and heading that direction in the first place was suicide because it meant battling the strongest flow of concrete.

He spun around, searching frantically for another option, fighting to stay on his feet as the gush of concrete increased around them. One more fall and it might prove fatal.

There was nothing on the opposite side of the pit but a sheer wall of earth, slowly disappearing under a thick gray blanket.

Shouts came from behind them up on the edge of the

pit but Jamie didn't dare look back. He threw himself behind Charlie, putting his body between her and Baker's men. If the fuckers were going to shoot them like fish in a barrel, they'd have to go through him to get to her.

Nudging her forward with his chest, he said a silent prayer, his heart in his throat as she took an unsteady step forward, the wet concrete sucking at their feet. He steeled himself, bracing for the burn of the bullets as they struck his body—

Gunfire erupted behind him.

He flinched, expecting to feel the burn of hot metal punching into his flesh.

It didn't happen.

He and Charlie both half-turned to look back, and the sight before them shot a yell of triumph and hope out of his taped mouth. Two men with rifles were crouched behind the cab of a concrete truck, firing at Baker and his men, who had scattered to return fire from behind the car they'd driven here in.

One of the men behind the concrete truck cab shifted, and a shaft of late afternoon sun hit his face. Jamie could have cried in gratitude.

Easton.

Relief and hope blasted through him. He didn't know how the hell his teammates had found them, and he didn't fucking care at the moment. His only priority was getting Charlie out of this death trap.

Nudging her with his shoulder, he motioned with his head toward the ramp and immediately took the lead, staying between her and the shooting.

Head down, he charged toward the ramp as fast as he could, fighting his way through the tangled mass of rebar and swirling concrete. It was up to his knees now, making every step a separate struggle as it sucked and pulled at his legs and feet.

His right shoe slipped. He stumbled on another piece

of rebar, almost fell but managed to regain his balance and keep going.

The volume of fire up above remained sporadic but Jamie didn't slow, didn't even risk glancing up to see what was happening, all his focus on getting to that ramp before one of Baker's men could take another shot at them.

A small river of dirt cascaded down the ramp. Jamie glanced up. Easton was right there near the end of the rapidly crumbling ramp, stretching out a hand for him, rifle slung across his back. "Come on, come on!" he yelled at them, face set in grim lines.

Jamie's right foot hit the hard-packed ramp, inches above the rising tide of concrete. Easton grabbed his shoulder, pulled hard to help him get onto the ramp, then planted a hand between Jamie's shoulder blades and shoved him forward. Jamie caught his balance and scrambled up the steep earthen path, Charlie's frantic voice floating up to him.

"Easton! What—"

"Don't talk, just run! Logan's got us covered." The sweet sound of an M4 firing punctuated his words.

Jamie's chest heaved as he finally reached solid ground, his legs burning. He rushed straight over behind the truck cab and crouched down next to Logan.

"You okay?" his teammate asked over the noise, just before pulling the trigger.

Jamie couldn't answer, his gaze pinned to where Easton was shoving Charlie over the lip of the pit. The moment she made it behind the cover of the truck's front tires he closed his eyes, his entire body sagging in relief.

Then Easton was behind him, cutting his hands free with a KA-BAR he pulled from his vest. Jamie ripped the fucking tape off his mouth and instantly reached for Charlie. She was on her knees beside him as Easton cut her wrists free.

Jamie took her face in his hands, forced that wide brown gaze to his as he wiped concrete from her cheeks. "Are you okay?" Logan fired another burst, keeping Baker's men pinned down.

Her face crumpled, her eyes flooding with tears. But she nodded. "Are you?"

"I'm okay. The bullet missed me." *Barely.* He turned to Easton, amped, every cell in his body dying to fight back. "Give me a fucking weapon."

Easton reached beneath the truck and dragged out a duffel. "Got you both covered."

Jamie fished out an M4 and slammed a mag into place, handed it to Charlie before readying his own weapon. Her hands shook but she took it without a word and put the sling around her body. God he wanted to kiss her. Hold her, squeeze her so tight she'd never feel scared again.

But first he was going to help take down the bastards who had almost killed them.

"Sitrep," he said to his teammates, moving at a crouch toward the front bumper while Easton and Logan maintained their sights on the enemy.

"Two down, Baker and two others still hidden on the far side of that second car," Logan answered, sighting down the barrel of his weapon. "Hamilton and the rest of the boys are en route and we've got a response team on the way. You good to go, or what?"

Chances were their backup wouldn't arrive in time to be of any real help in taking down Baker, but the four of them armed with rifles against three men with pistols? Baker didn't have a prayer of making it out of here. "Yeah, I'm good to go. And Baker's mine."

"Baker belongs to whoever gets the best angle," Easton fired back, moving to Logan's right. "Helo landed about a hundred yards to our two o'clock a few minutes ago," he added.

Baker's getaway vehicle. "Let's make sure he doesn't reach it." The bastard was going to do serious time and spill every last one of his ugly secrets to investigators.

"Roger that." Easton ducked back as a bullet pinged off the bumper.

"I see him."

At Charlie's announcement Jamie spun around to look behind him. His brave *pequeña* was lying flat on her stomach to her brother's right, peeking beneath the undercarriage of the truck at Baker's car, rifle to her shoulder.

"Baker?" he asked her, inching closer while Logan and Easton maintained their positions.

"Yeah, he's working his way toward the trunk. I don't have a clear shot, not even of his legs."

More bullets slammed into the side of the concrete truck. He stayed low, crept toward her while his teammates maintained their positions. "He's gonna make a break for the helo."

"We'll stop him." Her voice was so full of conviction, he couldn't help but smile.

"We're a great team." He ran his hand over the length of her hair, the ends caked in concrete. "But I want you to stay here with Logan and your brother."

Charlie turned her head to look up at him and nailed him with the most pissed-off look he'd ever seen from her. "Not a fucking chance. I'll go with you and we'll get him together. That asshole is going to pay for what he did, and I want to help take him down."

The volume of fire from Baker's men suddenly increased. The argument ready on the tip of Jamie's tongue was drowned out by a barrage of bullets slamming into the side of the truck, and into the ground. He grabbed Charlie's upper arm and hauled her to her feet behind the second set of tires just as rounds punched into the dirt mere feet from where she'd been lying.

"Baker's making a break for it," Easton shouted over the noise, ducked down behind the cab for cover. His gaze shifted from Charlie to Jamie, and he gave a nod. "You go after him. We'll cover you."

Jamie nodded. "Roger." He studied Charlie's face for a moment. "Sure? You're barefoot." Not to mention she'd been through hell already. But he trusted her ability and didn't want her to feel like he didn't see her as an equal.

Her jaw set. "Yes."

"Okay," he said to Easton. "You count it down."

Not wasting a second, he yanked Charlie with him and rushed behind the cover of the rear tires, barely making it there before more rounds peppered the rear of the truck, kicking up sprays of dirt and gravel.

As soon as it stopped he darted a peek around the back end of the truck. Baker was indeed hauling ass across the road and into the field beyond it, where the helo waited, rotors turning.

Jamie reached back, grabbed Charlie's left hand and placed it on his right shoulder. "You tell me when you're ready."

She shifted behind him, then squeezed, signaling her readiness.

"Three," Easton said behind them. "Two…one… *Go*."

His teammates stood up and rained a stream of suppressive fire at Baker's men, keeping them pinned behind the car. Jamie burst out from behind the truck and ran after Baker, his focus divided between shielding Charlie and not losing sight of his target. The son of a bitch was already partway across the field, the sloping terrain making a shot impossible from this distance.

Charlie was two steps behind him, running flat out in spite of her bare feet, while Logan and Easton kept the shooters busy.

Jamie locked his attention on Baker, his gaze glued to the back of that white tux jacket that stood out like a flag of surrender, and charged forward, weapon at the ready.

Time's up, asshole.

Chapter Fifteen

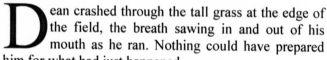

Dean crashed through the tall grass at the edge of the field, the breath sawing in and out of his mouth as he ran. Nothing could have prepared him for what had just happened.

One minute he'd been savoring the demise of the two people who were responsible for sending him on the run, and the next, two men had burst out of one of the concrete trucks and opened fire on him and his men.

It didn't matter now. As long as he got away.

His helicopter sat in the middle of the field, rotors turning, his pilot ready to whisk him away and out of range of fire.

He risked a glance behind him, his heart stuttering when he saw Jamie and Charlie chasing after him, armed with rifles. They were both covered in concrete, looking like gray ghosts coming to exact their revenge. Either one of them could easily have killed him from this distance, but that's not what they wanted.

No, they wanted to capture him and hand him over to the feds so he could be interrogated and imprisoned.

He refused to let that happen.

Whirling, pistol in hand, he fired off three shots.

Jamie ducked but didn't slow, just kept coming after him, and Charlie stayed right on his heels.

Dean fired three more times, then turned around and veered to the right, heading down a small incline in the terrain. A hot, searing pain bit into his left shoulder, an instant before the rifle's report rang out. He yelled as the agony spread through him, fell to his knees and struggled up once more, determined to get to his chopper.

The field dipped, allowing him some measure of protection as he ran, the pain making him light-headed. Close now. All he had to do was make it another fifty yards.

He veered left, then left again, before turning right and zigzagging his way toward the aircraft, hoping it would make him too difficult a target for his pursuers.

Up ahead, the details of the helicopter became clear. The gold stripe along its side became distinct, along with the letters painted onto its deep red body.

Another shot rang out behind him.

He cringed, heard the whine of the bullet as it sizzled past him, a leap of terror stealing the breath from his lungs.

He couldn't stop. Couldn't risk slowing down or turning around to fire again, and he was almost out of bullets now. Might have one or two shots left, he wasn't sure, and he needed to conserve them.

His legs were curiously numb, the pain in his left shoulder like fiery needles tearing into his flesh. *Almost there. You can make it.*

The pilot became distinct to him in the cockpit. He could see the man's face clearly, and a measure of relief shot through him. Allan had been his private pilot for years, would get him out of here.

Allan was talking on a cell phone as he watched him

run. He lowered it, and their gazes locked. Then Allan raised something in his hands.

A rifle. Pointed right at Dean through the open side window.

Dean slowed, instinctively ducked. But in that split second as he stared at the man who had flown him wherever he wanted to go for the past four years, Dean realized that Allan wasn't aiming the rifle at the two people chasing him.

Allan was aiming at *him*.

Electric terror forked through him. He yanked his pistol upward, preparing to fire.

A bullet slammed into his chest.

White-hot agony engulfed him as he dropped to his knees, slumped to his side. He opened his mouth to suck in air, but couldn't get any. His lungs weren't working.

His right arm was limp, unresponsive as he tried to reach for the gun, just inches from his outstretched fingers. A spreading pool of blood covered the grass. His blood. Because Allan had shot him.

Over the scream of denial locked in his throat, over the hideous anguish, the sound of the helicopter's engines powering up penetrated his brain. He opened and closed his mouth like a landed fish, starved for air, his eyes bulging from the lack of oxygen.

As the gray fog began to close in on him, he had only one thought.

Someone higher up the cartel food chain had ordered this.

****

Baker was down and he wasn't moving. Because his own pilot had just fucking shot him with a rifle.

Was he one of theirs? Someone sent by the DEA maybe?

Charlie kept running after Jamie as the helicopter nosed forward, locking her jaw at the pain stabbing through the soles of her bare feet. The rotor wash hit them. She leaned forward, squinted to minimize the dust and grit blowing into her eyes.

When Jamie reached Baker, he paused to kick the fallen pistol out of reach, then dropped to one knee facing the fleeing helo and raised his rifle. Charlie dropped next to him, panting, her entire body juiced with an overflow of adrenaline. Baker's chest had a golf ball-sized hole in it, just to the right of center. He was still alive, his eyes half-open, but judging by the slight movement in his chest and the pool of blood forming around him, he wouldn't be for long.

Fuck that. I want you to answer for what you've done.

She hadn't risked all this for him to die and take all his dirty secrets with him. She wanted him to live, so that the DEA and FBI could spend months cracking him, and then have the satisfaction of knowing he was rotting inside a prison cell for the rest of his life.

Leaning over him, she managed to wrench off his tux jacket, then wadded it up and shoved it against the wound in his chest. Those glassy brown eyes rolled toward her, focused for a moment, his face a kind of bluish-gray color.

"You don't get to die, you son of a bitch," she snarled at him over the noise of the helo. "Not unless it's in jail."

His eyes went unfocused again, his head lolling toward the helicopter.

She jumped when a gunshot pierced the sound of the helo's engine. Glancing up, she saw the pilot had swung the aircraft around to hover about twenty feet off the ground to fire at them.

Okay, the pilot wasn't one of them.

Next to her, Jamie had already taken aim. Before she could reach for her own weapon, he fired twice.

His bullets smashed through the cockpit windshield. Blood spattered over it.

The aircraft swung wildly to the right and lurched toward the ground like a wounded animal. Jamie was on his feet now, circling around in a wide arc, following its movement. It angled forward, the engines still screaming, nose tipping toward the earth.

Charlie stood frozen as it limped along, never pulling up, inching closer and closer to the surface of the field.

The tip of the main rotor caught the ground. Dirt and plant matter sprayed in the air as the blades chewed up the field, then the momentum flipped the aircraft onto its back.

Charlie gasped and took a step back. It spun around in a deranged circle like a dying bird. The tail plunged down, sending it into a roll, engines still going full tilt. It flipped twice then hit the ground with a bone-shaking thud, and burst into flames.

Jamie grabbed her and dragged her down to her knees, wrapping his arms around her, angling his body to shield her. A blast of heat rolled over them both.

As soon as he eased up she looked around his shoulder at the fiery wreckage, the acrid scent of smoke stinging her nose. She didn't have time to process more than the thick black plume of smoke boiling into the air before Jamie caught her face between his hands, his eyes delving into hers. "Are you all right?"

It was over.

She nodded, put her hands on his cheeks. "You?" He was covered in concrete too, blood dripping from the cut above his eye, which was swelling shut again. But they were both alive.

"Yeah." He hauled her into his arms, crushed her to his chest, his face pressed to her hair. "Christ, Trouble. *Christ.*"

Charlie clung to him in return, closed her eyes and

just held on, absorbing the warm vitality of him, the rush of elation that they were both alive, both safe. Then the subtle vibrations of approaching footfalls behind them pierced her awareness.

Glancing back, she found her brother and Logan racing toward them, rifles slung across their backs. The other shooters must be dead then. And over the roar of the fire she caught the wail of sirens. *Finally.*

Her brother skidded to his knees next to her and grabbed her from Jamie. "Charlie," he rasped out, locking those strong, familiar arms around her, one hand cradling the back of her head protectively.

For some reason, his embrace crumbled the last of her defenses. The brave front she'd been putting on melted away in a single heartbeat, leaving her raw and exposed and…vulnerable. She wrapped her arms around his back and hugged him hard, her face scrunching. The tears she'd fought so hard to hide came flooding out, no matter how hard she tried to hold them back.

"Ah, sweetheart," he murmured, shifting to nestle her closer into his body. "You're okay now. It's gonna be okay."

She nodded, hid her face so that Jamie couldn't see her falling apart. But she felt him there, hovering behind her. A hand stroked over her hair and she knew without looking that it was his.

Without stopping to think or question her actions, she pushed away from Easton and reached for Jamie instead, grabbing fistfuls of his ruined and blood-stained tux shirt and burying her face in the side of his neck. He drew her up off the ground and settled her into his lap, closing his arms around her without a word.

At least to her.

"I got her," he said quietly to Easton. "You guys go ahead and deal with the entourage."

The sirens were getting louder now. Whoever was

coming would want to know what had happened, and someone would have to try to stabilize Baker—

She jerked her head up, wiped at her eyes as she peered over Jamie's broad shoulder. "Is he—"

"Dead."

No. She slumped, laid her forehead against Jamie's shoulder. "I only had a few seconds to transmit from his laptop. I don't even know if I got anything," she mumbled.

"You got some," Logan said as he pushed to his feet beside Baker's body. "Taylor was trying to work on it before we got the emergency signal from Jamie."

Well, she hoped she'd transmitted something useful, because with both Baker and his pilot dead, they weren't getting any other intel from them. Dammit!

As Logan walked away Charlie took several deep breaths to settle herself, then sat back and wiped at her dirty face. Jamie gazed into her eyes for a moment and must have been satisfied with what he saw, because he stood and helped her up.

He walked her a short distance away from Baker's body. Easton was already at the road, talking with the cops and agents that were now swarming the scene.

"Where did they all come from?" she asked Jamie.

"Team had them waiting as backup."

She looked up at him, brushed at some of the concrete clinging to the edge of his battered face. "I thought my heart would stop when I saw you tied to the chair in that room."

"Yeah, mine did the same when I saw you in the doorway." He shook his head once, a grin tugging at his mouth. "I still can't believe what you did. Wait, yes I can."

Despite the horrific situation they'd just gone through, she cracked a laugh. "It just came to me and I went with it. Figured I had nothing to lose by trying."

"And you saved our asses in the process." He dragged her into another tight hug, then cupped her chin in his big hand and bent his head to brush his lips over hers. "You really okay?"

She forced a nod. "Just glad we're both alive." And grateful that she would get the chance to say all the things she should have last night.

A smile lit his eyes. He kissed her gently, then bent and scooped her up in his arms.

"What are you doing?" she protested. "I'm not hurt."

"You're all banged up and your feet are probably a mess. So I'm carrying you to the nearest ambulance to get you checked over. Don't bother arguing."

Embarrassed, but secretly liking that he would do this for her, she looped her arms around his neck and looked toward the road. Her brother was staring at them intently. Had he seen Jamie kiss her? She didn't care.

Tipping her head back to look up at Jamie, she savored the feel of his arms around her. "When this whole mess is over, I want some quality alone time with you." Once the physical needs they'd denied for too long were taken care of, they were going to talk about their future.

Jamie shifted her in his arms and kept walking toward the mass of flashing lights clogging the road. "That's a promise, Trouble. You couldn't keep me away tonight if you tried."

Chapter Sixteen

━━━━◇◇◇◇◇━━━━

Jamie scrubbed the spare T-shirt Logan had given him over his face, then stripped off the ruined tux shirt and slid the soft cotton over his head. "I feel better already."

"You don't look better," Logan remarked, leaning against the back of the van he and the others had arrived in. Easton and Taylor were with Charlie while she got checked out by the paramedics.

A familiar whumping noise approached overhead. Jamie glanced up in time to see the Blackhawk's silhouette appear over a line of trees on the distant ridge.

"That'll be Hamilton and the rest of the boys," Logan said.

The helo circled once, then came in for a landing on the edge of the farmer's field. Its wheels touched down and the engines began the shutdown mode. The side door slid open and their team leader jumped out first, then the other five members of FAST Bravo, all kitted up and in tac gear.

"Now that's a sight for sore eyes," Jamie said to

Logan.

"Wish they'd shown up an hour ago, though."

"For real."

Jamie walked over and met Hamilton on the road. "Thanks for coming," he said with a wry grin.

Hamilton shook his hand and clapped him on the shoulder. "Good to see you. Just sorry we didn't get here faster."

FAST hadn't been part of this operation beyond him, Easton and Logan being involved in various ways. That Hamilton and the others had all hopped a helo and flown up here to save his ass in the first place meant the world to Jamie. "It's okay. Turned out well in the end."

Hamilton nodded, shook Logan's hand and glanced around. "How's Charlie?"

"Good. No serious injuries. Easton and Taylor are with her now."

His team leader's dark gray eyes crinkled as he half-smiled. "That Colebrook warrior blood is damn strong stuff."

It sure as hell was.

"You need anything?"

"Nah, I'm good." *Just anxious to get all the statements, debriefings and meetings over with as fast as possible so I can get back to NYC and spend the rest of the night with Charlie.* He smiled at the rest of his teammates as they came up to him, received man-hugs and back claps from the guys.

"Man, leave it to you to get into the shit on your own," Kai said, shaking his head at him as the others gathered around them. "You okay, brother?"

"Yeah. Hell of a day, though."

He cracked a crooked grin. "Beer and a steak dinner on me once we get back to Virginia."

Being offered a meal by the team's big guy—and cheapest guy—was the highest form of compliment.

"Deal."

Hamilton stood off to the left, talking with another member of the taskforce. When they both turned toward him, Jamie knew the socializing was over. He inwardly groaned, shot a quick look over at the ambulance where Charlie was still with the paramedics.

She was sitting on the gurney in the back, a blanket around her shoulders as she spoke to them. Even covered in concrete residue, his heart beat faster at the sight of her. Her strength and bravery amazed him. She was absolutely the woman he wanted at his side for the rest of his life.

Whether or not she wanted that place was another story. One he needed to get the answer to as soon as possible, because there was no way he could keep his distance from her after this. Not with everything they'd been through together. If he had to let her go after tonight, it would shred him.

"Rodriguez."

He glanced over at Hamilton. "Yeah, coming."

It took several hours to go over everything with the taskforce leaders, investigative team and forensics people. Per standard procedure they split him and Charlie up to get their individual stories about the sequence of events, taking them separately around the site to question them. Once that was done they had a meeting with the taskforce people, and Charlie was finally offered a ride back to the city with her boss.

She looked over her shoulder at him on the way to the waiting vehicle, her eyes full of questions. He gave her a reassuring smile and nodded once. Tonight was so happening. He'd do whatever it took to get to her.

She smiled back, then turned around and walked toward the SUV.

Jamie was still talking to investigators twenty minutes later when Hamilton finally came over to break it up. "You've got what you need already. My guys need to eat, get cleaned up and then get some sleep," he said, his tone brooking no argument. "Anything you need from them can be handled in the morning at this point, right?"

Damn, Jamie loved that guy.

The investigators hurriedly wrapped everything up. Jamie said goodbye to Hamilton and the five teammates who had flown up with him, then headed back to the van. Easton and Logan were waiting there for him.

Together they watched the Blackhawk power up and lift into the twilit sky. As it soared overhead, one of the guys—probably Kai—leaned out of the open door and gave them a sustained one-fingered salute during the flyby.

Grinning, Jamie turned toward the others.

"Shotgun," Logan said as Easton headed around the other side to get in the driver's seat.

Jamie hustled around and stopped him before he could open the door. "Can I have a second?" He needed to talk to his buddy in private before they hit the road. What he had to say had been weighing on his mind and he didn't want to put it off any longer.

Easton regarded him for a long moment, then gave a nod and shut the door. They walked a few yards away from the van for privacy and faced the pit where Jamie and Charlie had almost met their demise a few hours earlier. It seemed surreal now.

"So, what's up?" Easton asked, hands on hips.

There was no easy way to say it, but he had to. He couldn't keep this from his best friend anymore. Easton was like a brother to him, and roles reversed, he'd want to know if Easton was involved with Jamie's sister. "It's Charlie."

His friend's expression never changed. "Okay."

"I don't want her to be alone tonight."

"Me neither. Taylor's gonna stay with her until I get there—"

"I'm staying with her."

Easton blinked once, his gaze sharpening. "Really." He paused a beat. "So you two are together? Or…?" He left the last bit dangling, but the annoyance in his tone made it clear how he felt about that latter possibility.

Shit, he hadn't meant for it to come across like that. Jamie wiped a hand over the lower half of his face and sighed. "Look. I've got…feelings for her."

"Feelings," Easton repeated with a frown, folding his arms over his chest.

Yeah, he had to man up and say it. "Straight up?"

There was a hard glint in his buddy's eyes. "I'd prefer it, yeah."

Well damn, he couldn't very well tell Easton that he loved her, could he? Not before telling her first. There was a certain protocol he needed to follow there. "I…"

Easton raised an eyebrow as the awkwardness hung there. "Yeah?" he prompted.

Jamie sighed. "It's been building for a year now."

"Building."

Jamie nodded but didn't elaborate. The less said right now, the better, so long as Easton knew the gist.

Another frown, this one more ominous than the last. "So you two have been…" He grimaced and shook his head. "No, forget I said that. I don't wanna know. Christ, Rodriguez. My *sister*?"

"I know. But I'm serious about her."

Easton scratched the side of his jaw, seemed to consider that for a long moment. "She feel the same way about you?"

Jamie hid a wince. The truth hurt, man. "I don't know yet, but I'm hoping to convince her to give us a shot." Starting tonight.

His friend huffed out a breath, shook his head. "Yeah, looking back, I guess I can't say I'm all that surprised. She was always asking me about you during our last deployment, and after that 407 went down today she wanted you, not me."

"And you don't know how fucking happy that made me," Jamie said with a chuckle. Her reaching for him rather than her brother for comfort was huge.

Easton cracked a grin, then sobered. "So what happens if things…don't work out with you guys? I don't want it to be awkward. I want to still be able to hang out with you both and spend time at the farm together or whatever."

"Guess I'll cross that bridge if I come to it." But the mere thought of Charlie turning him down put a lump of dread in the pit of his stomach.

Easton clapped him on the shoulder. "Okay, man. I appreciate you telling me."

"Thanks for not knocking my teeth down my throat."

His lips quirked. "Only because you said you're serious. But honestly? I can see it. You two, together. It's pretty damn cool, actually. I hope it works out."

"Thanks, man." Relief slid through him, and he felt better for having said his piece.

"So. Should we get going? Guess you're anxious to get back to…." He grimaced again and gave a dramatic gulp. "My sister."

More than you can imagine, brother. "Yeah, let's go." He was desperate to finish what they'd started.

And hopefully begin something far more.

****

Charlie shifted on the sofa and willed her mind to stop spinning, to no avail. It was after midnight now. She'd been back at the apartment for a couple hours now, after doing more interviews and answering questions until her brain turned numb. They'd let her shower first, thankfully, allowing her ample time to scrub off all the concrete she'd been covered with. The drug Baker had given her had long since left her system, but she still felt stupid for accepting that beer in the first place. Investigators were executing various search warrants at Baker's place right now, on the hunt for the laptop, other evidence and whatever security video footage they could get.

In the meantime, Jamie had been stuck in separate meetings with the rest of the taskforce at another location, but Taylor had been here with her. Charlie had sent her home an hour ago, since Taylor had been struggling to keep her eyes open.

But mostly because she wanted to be alone with Jamie the instant he got here. He'd promised he'd come, so he would be here as soon as he could.

She sat bolt upright on the sofa when she heard the key in the lock, heart thudding.

The lock clicked and the knob began to turn.

She bounded to her feet, ignoring the aches in her body where the bruises throbbed, and was already halfway across her apartment living room when the door opened. A soft, desperate sound came from her throat when Jamie appeared in the doorway, his dark-honey gaze colliding with hers.

He'd showered at some point and changed into jeans and a T-shirt, and someone had put a Steri-Strip over the cut on his eyebrow. The rest of his face was slightly battered and she wanted to kiss every mark on his skin better.

She'd had a lot of time to think since leaving Long Island. Enough to crystalize what she wanted most going forward.

And he was standing right in front of her.

She launched herself at him. He caught her with a soft grunt, and hoisted her upward as she wound her arms and legs around him. Burying her face in the side of his neck, Charlie dragged in a deep breath, drawing his masculine scent deep into her lungs. "God, I've missed you."

Charlie had never needed anyone before. Not like this. She'd come so close to losing him today, to dying. It had been more than a wakeup call. Everything she'd felt for him had become clear, along with the decision she'd made.

She was done with hiding behind the fear of potentially losing him one day, the way her father had lost her mother. The way Jamie's father was about to lose his wife.

Life was too damn short and she wasn't wasting another moment of it hiding behind excuses or lies she'd been telling herself all these years. The hours she'd spent waiting for him to come to her had been endless. Now that she had him, she wasn't letting him go.

Jamie eased her head back to look down at her. His gaze was like molten amber, so hot it burned as it dipped down to her mouth, and the intensity coming from him sucked the air from her lungs.

Twining her fingers in his hair, she lifted up as his lips closed over hers in a scorching, bone-melting kiss that lit up every nerve in her body. His free hand locked in her hair, holding her head still while his tongue stroked along hers, his other arm banded tight around her hips to keep her in place. Charlie poured her heart into the kiss as he carried her through the living room and into the darkened bedroom, not bothering to shut the door.

Her back hit the mattress. She shimmied her legs up higher around his back as he lowered his weight onto her, moaned into his mouth as the hard outline of his erection made contact with the needy flesh between her thighs. She'd wanted this man for so damn long, but it was far more than that now.

She *needed* him, and that was a new, terrifying first.

She'd never made herself vulnerable to a man before. Not really. But pinned beneath his hard weight, the waves of emotion kept battering at her, threatening to tear her apart. She loved him. Would have died to save him today, and he'd been ready to do the same for her. It choked her up.

"Need you," he muttered against her mouth, his kisses hard, urgent.

A shockwave of hunger tore through her. With greedy hands they stripped each other, seams popping as they tugged and yanked clothing out of the way and tossed it aside. She had to unwind her legs for him to peel her pants and panties off, then gasped and went still when he locked his strong, warm hands around her ankles and held them.

Slowly, inexorably he drew her legs farther apart, his hot stare going to the swollen place between them. "Lie still," he commanded in a low voice, then leaned forward, lowering his upper body until his face was directly between her open thighs.

Charlie's heart skipped as she lay there beneath him, watching his face. His expression was focused, determined as he bent toward her aching flesh. The warmth of his breath washed over her. A whimper locked in her throat, her hands curling into the bedding. *Don't make me wait another second.*

His lips brushed over her in a soft, teasing kiss. She raised her hips, impatient, needing him so badly she ached, a knot of raw emotion lodged in her throat. Those golden eyes lifted to hers and he nuzzled her, parted his lips to graze his tongue along her sensitive folds.

A ragged gasp sucked air into her lungs. Charlie bit her lip and kept watching, dying for the moment when he finally gave her what she wanted. What she needed more than she needed oxygen. Not simply release, but the feeling of being possessed by this intense, sexy and brave man.

Jamie growled low in his throat and began his erotic exploration, stroking and sucking at her folds, the quivering bundle of nerves at the top of her sex. Pleasure rose like a dark wave inside her, reaching higher and higher, pushing her to the precipice. His wicked, torturous tongue swirled around her aching clit, then his lips closed around it.

Sweet, delicious suction surrounded those sizzling nerve endings. She bowed up, crying his name, a breathless plea for him not to stop.

Strong hands closed around her hips, held tight for a long moment before one slid upward to cup her breast, his thumb and forefinger rolling her nipple. Hot, electric pleasure seared through her. Then his tongue was pushing into her, delving.

She blindly reached for his head, panting. "Jamie—"

He made a low, negative sound and grasped her wrists, pulling them free of his hair as he sat up on his knees.

She opened her mouth to protest but the look on his face made the words die on her tongue. His expression was fierce, so full of longing and need that her heart clenched. She was so in love with this man, didn't know how she could ever go on without him. Her stubborn pride be damned—she'd give him anything he wanted, including a shot at forever. "I want to feel you come around me when I'm buried deep inside you."

Yes. "Come here," she murmured, and sat up to reach for his shoulders.

He caught her by the upper arms, held her still for a moment, then pushed her backward. Only when she was lying flat did he allow her to touch him, taking her hands and placing them in the center of his chest.

She followed the contours of muscle with her palms and fingertips, reveled in his strength and vitality before trailing down over his rigid stomach to where his swollen cock stood so proud against his lower belly.

The instant she curled her fingers around him he groaned and bowed his head, his features tightening in near pain. He allowed her to stroke and squeeze for a few moments, then took her hands and pulled them away from his body, bringing them up to rest on either side of her head.

Staring up at him in the dimness, Charlie took it one step further.

As he released her and sat back on his haunches, she held his gaze and slowly raised her arms over her head, wrapped her fingers around the underside of the headboard. Silently signaling her surrender, giving him her body and her submission. She knew he needed this, secretly craved this, and she was willing to stretch her boundaries for him.

Because she trusted him, and because she wanted to experience this kind of total surrender with him. Laying herself bare for him on a level she never had with anyone else. Terrifying and thrilling at the same time.

Jamie's eyes flared hot like a match strike and he sucked in a breath. With one hand he drew gentle fingers over her cheek, down the length of her nose and across her lips, his thumb lingering there. She kissed it, let her tongue tease the pad of it, and a slow, erotic smile curved his mouth.

He leaned over to grab something from the floor but she was too busy staring at that powerful male physique with all the bunching muscles to care what he was doing. God, her heart was pounding.

When he sat up again he already had a condom in hand. She licked her lips, all but squirming in anticipation as he rolled it down the length of his erection, giving himself a slow stroke that made her core clench. She'd wanted Jamie for so damn long, had never expected him to steal her heart so completely, and part of her couldn't believe she was actually about to have him.

In a slow, deliberate movement he settled the head of his cock against her folds and rocked forward, gliding across her pulsing clit. Over and over he repeated the motion, one hand smoothing upward to cup her breast and play with her nipple. Sensation zinged through her body, a moan rippling out of her.

She curled her fingers tighter around the bottom of the headboard, wanting to touch him, to drag him down on top of her, but she knew he wanted this. So she lay there quivering, biting her lip as he finally eased forward, bracing his forearms on either side of her head. His stare drilled into hers as he flexed his hips, burying his length inside her in one slow, inexorable thrust.

Charlie gasped and arched, clinging to the headboard. He was so thick, stretching her, soothing the empty ache he'd created in her.

Framing her face between his hands, Jamie lowered his mouth to hers, licked into her mouth as he remained locked deep inside her. Her inner muscles clenched around him, greedy for more, and she couldn't help twining her thighs around his, needing that anchor.

Her throat and chest were tight, a rush of emotion making her eyes burn. He kissed her slow and deep as he began to move, rocking gently, the angle of his strokes rubbing his pelvis against her throbbing clit.

Not enough. It was torture, even more than when he'd gone down on her. She was full, every slide of his cock stroking the sweet spot inside her, but she needed more direct friction against her clit. He was driving her crazy.

A frustrated sound came from the back of her throat. She locked her thighs harder around his, wriggling to find the contact she needed.

With a low chuckle, he slipped one hand between

them and rested his thumb alongside her clit. Not rubbing or circling the tender bud, just a tantalizing pressure against the edge.

Charlie mewled into his mouth and writhed in his hold, heart pounding and a fine sheen of sweat breaking out across her skin, fighting the urge to let go of the headboard and dig her fingers into his broad shoulders instead. He had her so close, just a few seconds of the right friction and she'd explode.

He continued to roll his hips against her in an almost lazy motion, his strokes growing a little harder each time. It took all her remaining control to keep her hands on the headboard.

She twisted her head to the side and opened her mouth to beg but then he moved his thumb, caressing just the right spot and the only sound that came out of her was a long, liquid moan of desperate bliss. This was so far beyond physical, the bond between them more intimate than anything she'd imagined.

Jamie was both tender and firm, maintaining complete control over her, demanding her surrender. His one hand stayed locked in her hair, his lips and tongue stroking hers while he drove into her in a smooth, steady rhythm, the thumb between her thighs making the pleasure burn like fire. The pressure grew and grew inside her until she was moaning and shaking, reaching for the orgasm that hovered so tantalizingly close.

"You're mine, Charlotte."

Nobody ever called her by her real name. She hated being called that. It was too girly.

And yet, from him in that dark, velvet voice so full of tender possessiveness…it sent her flying.

Blind with pleasure, overcome with emotion, she let go of the headboard and reached for him. Her grasping fingers dug deep into the bunching muscles in his shoulders as her orgasm hit.

Sharp, wild cries tore from her, her entire body bucking while he pinned her there and took her apart. The sweet waves went on and on until the touch between her thighs gently eased, leaving her to sag against the bed, panting, eyes closed.

And her heart was nothing but a puddle of mush nestled safely in his palms.

Jamie's mouth found hers once more, stroking, licking, both hands now cradling her head. "God, I love you," he whispered, still thick and hard inside her, each subtle shift of their bodies sending a glow of pleasure through her veins.

Her heart cracked wide open. "Love you too," she whispered, terror and elation whipsawing through her. She'd never said those words to any man outside her family before. But she'd never meant them more, or in this way. He owned her, body and soul. "So much."

Jamie's entire body shuddered. Actually shuddered at her words.

They were everything he'd wanted, and more than he'd dared hope for at this stage. And the way she'd just surrendered herself to him, her unspoken trust in the gesture, was the most precious gift he'd ever been given.

Mine. She's all mine. He would never let her walk away now. He'd do whatever it took to keep her.

Burying his face in the curve of her neck and shoulder, he nipped at her skin lightly, surging into her harder. The need for release was all-consuming, pounding at him because he was deep inside Charlie and she fucking owned him.

He pushed deeper yet, making low, guttural sounds of pleasure in the back of his throat that he had no control over whatsoever. Her muscles clenched around him, that tight squeeze increasing the friction and heat.

The best part was how Charlie cradled him to her,

holding him as close as she could, moving into each thrust, her legs clamping around his hips. His heart pounded out of control, threatened to burst as the sensations sharpened. She tightened her inner muscles around his cock, hummed in pleasure when he sucked in a breath and moaned against her skin.

God.

Fisting handfuls of her hair, squeezing, he sought his own release, the pleasure sizzling up his spine. He pressed as close to her as he could get, tighter still, then plunged deep, his muscles cording as his groans of ecstasy echoed around the room, his face buried against her sweet-smelling skin.

He didn't know how long he stayed there like that, buried to the hilt inside her, the frantic rhythm of his heart easing back to normal. She was still cradling him as though he was something precious she couldn't bear to let go of. It gave him hope.

Cool air washed over his damp back. He was heavy, should probably roll off her, but he couldn't summon the will to move. Being surrounded by her like this was pure heaven and he'd wanted it for so damn long.

But he wanted way more. Wanted everything she had to give, because he was ready to give her the same.

Her gentle fingers trailed over his shoulders, up the back of his neck to his head. She played with his hair for a few blissful minutes, then kissed his hot temple, turning his face to place tender butterfly kisses on each nick and bruise on his skin. "I was hoping it would be like that with you," she murmured finally, a smile in her voice.

Jamie braced himself on his forearms and raised his head to stare down at her. The light coming from the hallway through the open door illuminated her face perfectly. Her deep, chocolate-brown eyes gazed up at him, soft with trust and satisfaction.

And love.

He felt twelve fucking feet tall.

She shifted, lifted her head to brush a kiss over his lips. "You told me there was another reason why you wanted all or nothing with me. What was it?"

Was she considering it then? She'd told him she loved him, but was she willing to give him all of herself? His heart beat faster. "I lost a good buddy I'd met back in boot camp. Between that and my mom's diagnosis, I realized life's too short to settle. I want something real, something that will last. And I want it with you."

A slow, tender smile lifted the corners of her mouth. "Even though I'm trouble?"

"*Because* you're trouble." Unclenching his fists from her hair, he cradled her head in his hands, swept his thumbs back and forth across her bold cheekbones. "You said you love me."

Her dark eyes stared up into his, mysterious and deep. "Yeah, I did. And you said you love me. How about that."

"I do. I love you like crazy." He would have sacrificed himself in a heartbeat today if it meant saving her.

Her smile widened and she skimmed her hands over his upper back. "I think I like this romantic side of you."

She hadn't begun to see that side of him yet, and he was looking forward to showing it to her. A real date. Dinner out somewhere, then a romantic walk, complete with a full-on seduction long before he got her home, so that she was desperate to have him before he ever started peeling her clothes off.

Slowly, so she'd bite her lip and tremble with anticipation.

"No running, Trouble. It's way too late for that."

For a moment she hesitated, and he thought his heart might implode from the stress. Then she sighed and shook her head slightly. "No. No running. I'm all in."

He smiled so damn wide it was a wonder his face didn't split in half. "Glad you feel that way, because there was no damn way I was letting you go," he said, and took her mouth in a slow, possessive kiss, ready to give her another demonstration of the side benefits that came with being his.

Epilogue

Sugar Hollow, VA
Two weeks later

The creak of the wooden floor outside her room brought Charlie's eyes open from a decadent, delicious afternoon nap.

Couldn't be a family member coming down the hallway, since everyone knew exactly which old floorboard to avoid—a handy bit of knowledge for her and her brothers during their teenage years when they'd snuck in after curfew and tried to slip into their rooms without alerting their scary-ass father.

So it had to be Jamie coming toward her.

She rolled to her back in her childhood bed tucked under the eaves of her second-floor room in her father's house and stretched her arms over her head, a smile curving her mouth. The weeks since the ordeal in New York had flown by, and she'd recently returned to her duties full-time, after helping with the investigation.

With Baker and his pilot both dead, there hadn't been

a lot of intel to work with. Baker's laptop had been conspicuously absent from the property when the taskforce had gone in with the search warrant. No one knew where it was now, but it had likely been destroyed by one of Baker's men. The files she'd managed to send from it were sparse, and what was there was so heavily encrypted, Taylor's team was still working on cracking it.

Not only that, investigators were still trying to figure out why the pilot had killed Baker. Someone from the cartel must have ordered it, they just didn't know who.

Thankfully that was mostly behind her now. And she'd also traveled to southern California with Jamie ten days ago to meet his family. His mother was gravely ill, but her entire face had lit up when he'd walked into the house. It had put a lump in Charlie's throat, seeing how much they loved each other. Getting to know his family had only solidified her feelings that he was the man she wanted to spend the rest of her life with.

Her gaze fell on a framed picture of her and her mother. Charlie was about three, curled up in her lap while reading a story together, big smiles on both their faces at some funny part. A bittersweet feeling spread through her chest as she looked at it. *I miss you, Mama. I wish you'd have been able to meet Jamie. You'd have loved him.*

A soft knock on the door, then the knob turned and the door pushed open. Jamie was there in jeans and a T-shirt that hugged his muscular torso, his dark gold eyes warming to molten honey when he saw her sprawled out on the bed in her jeans and snug T-shirt. "Hey."

"Hey," she murmured, unable to keep the smile off her face. "You're early." He wasn't supposed to arrive until close to midnight.

"Couldn't wait to see you," he said, crossing the room to sit on the edge of the bed.

Her heart beat faster as she sat up and crawled into

his arms, nestling her head on his shoulder. "Mmm, you smell good."

He chuckled. "Yeah, because I smell like coffee. Easton's just making a fresh pot."

"He's a good brother," she said with a fond smile. Easton had been wholly supportive of her relationship with Jamie, and she loved that the two of them were so close.

"Did you tell your dad yet?"

"No." She'd only arrived a few hours ago, and her dad had been out working with the farrier. "And that's not something you *tell* my father, it's something you *ask* him."

He chuckled. "My brave-hearted *pequeña's* not so brave all of a sudden, huh?"

"He's my *dad*. And I'm not only his baby, I'm his only daughter." The man was a freaking legend around these parts. Hell, in the Marine Corps.

"You still want me to do it, then?"

"Yes. He's old-fashioned like that."

Jamie hummed and stroked a hand over her hair. "So, were you dreaming about me?"

"Maybe," she said in a sly tone, rubbing against his chest. "And it might have been naughty, because I'm feeling rather...tingly right now."

He growled deep in his chest and pulled her head away from his chest to plant a hard, possessive kiss on her lips. "Please say there's a spot we can ride out to later that will give us a good hour of privacy."

"Well, there might be." She had several in mind already. "I'll see what I can do. I believe I once offered to take you out...*riding*, last year," she added in a sultry tone.

"Such a tease." He released her and stood, held out an imperious hand. "Come on. I was instructed to come get you and bring you downstairs."

She set her hand in his, allowed him to pull her from the cozy nest she would rather spend the rest of the day in with him, and headed downstairs. The familiar sights and smells of home surrounded her, filling her with warmth. The deep tones of two of her brothers' voices drifted up from the kitchen.

Easton and Wyatt were both here. Only Brody—her middle brother—was missing, off on yet another mission with the FBI's Hostage Rescue Team. All the men in her family were former military and ridiculously alpha, but even though she'd chafed against their protective restrictions when she was younger, she wouldn't change any of them for the world.

"Hey, there's Sleeping Beauty," Easton remarked when she came into view. He was standing at the kitchen sink with a mug in hand, eyes glinting with humor.

"You got any of that left?"

"Nope, sorry, already poured the last cup," her eldest brother, Wyatt said, pouring the last dregs from the pot into her favorite mug. He had shorts on today, telling her he was way more comfortable letting people see his prosthetic leg than he had been even a few months ago. He wore his favorite T-shirt, a gift from Easton that read: *I had a blast in Afghanistan.*

Sometimes her brothers' sense of humor left something to be desired.

Charlie glared at Wyatt in outrage. "That's my mug."

"Is it?" He stared at her, raised the rim to his lips as though he intended to drink from it, and at the last moment grinned and handed it over. "I can be an asshole sometimes, I know, but I'm not that mean."

"Yeah, Austen's been good for you," she said with a smile, gratefully accepting the mug.

"I love how she melts when someone gives her coffee. Easton gave me that tip a few weeks back. It's come in handy a few times since," Jamie said.

"Eww, TMI," Wyatt muttered, and Easton laughed.

"We still having pizza for dinner?" Charlie asked.

"Nope. Austen got wind that you and Jamie were coming down for a visit, so she and Piper are at our place right now using every pot and pan in the kitchen to cook up a feast."

Charlie brightened. Austen and Piper in the kitchen together was a combination straight out of heaven. "Is Austen making her mama's mac 'n cheese?"

"I assume so, and Piper had brownies and lemon bars in the oven when I left."

"Oh, now I can't wait." She turned to Jamie, looped an arm around his waist and leaned into him. "I love family dinners, but even more now that you're here."

Before Jamie could utter a response her brothers let out a chorus of fake awwws and kissy noises. Charlie shot them a dirty look, fighting back a smile.

Then the kitchen door opened. A blur of white and chestnut-brown fur exploded into the room, heading straight for her.

"Grits! How's my cute little buddy doing, huh?" she asked, bending down just as the little Cavalier King Charles Spaniel jumped up to place his front paws on her thigh and cover her face with puppy kisses, his feathery white tail swishing back and forth in a blur.

"He's doing great," Wyatt said, sounding like a proud father. "Spoiled as hell and loving every minute of it. He helps me out with the shelter dogs we select for our therapy dog program. You wouldn't believe how fast some of those dogs come out of their shells when he's around."

"Oh yes, I would." And the artificial back leg hadn't slowed the little guy down one bit. "He's so freaking adorable. Aren't you, Gritsy?" she gushed, ruffling both his long, floppy ears.

Grits cocked his head to the side and gazed up at her

with total adoration, his tongue lolling out the side of his mouth in a doggy smile.

"So you're up finally."

She glanced up to find her father standing in the kitchen doorway, leaning on his cane, one side of his handsome face drooping slightly. The stroke had left its mark on him physically, but her old man was a fighter and still sharp as a damn whip. He was still here, still capable, and wasn't leaving this earth anytime soon, thank God.

"Hey, Daddy." Grinning, she got up and walked over to hug him.

He wrapped one arm around her to return the embrace, then jerked his chin at Jamie. "So, you're back. You here for her, or Easton?"

"Both," Jamie answered diplomatically.

Her father grunted and patted her back, then stepped back and shuffled into the kitchen, his faithful retired narco-Bassett Hound, Sarge, at his heels. "When's dinner?"

Wyatt checked his watch. "Thirty-two minutes."

"You boys go ahead," he said to Wyatt and Easton. "I'll catch a ride with these two." He nodded at her and Jamie. "But first…" He turned his head, that hazel gaze that had been known to make grown Marines piss their pants landing squarely on Jamie. "You look like you've got something on your mind, son. Maybe you and me should have a little talk before we go to supper." Without waiting, he turned and shuffled his way toward his study.

Charlie bit her lip to keep from smiling as Easton and Wyatt both snickered. It wasn't a secret that she and Jamie were together now, and that both of them were ready to take things to the next level. By moving in together.

She just hadn't told her father that yet.

Jamie grinned good-naturedly as Easton came over to slap him on the back and offered a, "Good luck, brother."

220

"Thanks. I—" Jamie stopped, did a double-take as he craned his neck around to see her father in his study, then snapped his head around and looked at her with an incredulous expression. "Is he seriously cleaning a shotgun right now?" he whispered.

She winced. Her father could be so ridiculous sometimes, but she loved him anyway. "Pretty sure, yeah."

Wyatt chuckled under his breath and grabbed his black Stetson from the kitchen table. "Much as I'd love to stay and watch this, my fiancée will have my hide if I'm not home when dinner's supposed to start." He slapped Jamie on the shoulder on his way by. "Guess we won't wait, but we'll save some for you guys."

Jamie looked at her, alarm in his eyes as the kitchen door swung closed behind her brothers, leaving them alone. "Are you...coming in there with me?" he asked, looking adorably hopeful and confused and alarmed all at the same time.

"Nope. Sorry, big guy. You have to pass this rite of passage on your own. Just remember I love you, and that I'm worth it." Lifting up on her toes, she smacked a kiss on his lips then gently pushed him toward the study where her father was fiendishly cleaning a barrel of his shotgun, albeit awkwardly now that he had only limited use of one arm.

Love and pride overwhelmed her as she watched Jamie straighten his shoulders and walk toward what was no doubt going to be one of the most uncomfortable experiences of his life.

"Slide the pocket doors shut and have a seat," her former USMC gunny sergeant father said gruffly without looking up from his work.

Jamie hesitated a moment, then pivoted around to pull the oak doors closed. Through the opening, his eyes met hers. She grinned and blew him a kiss, and he gave her a mock scowl before pulling the doors shut.

Poor guy.

Smiling to herself, she took her coffee and went over to sit at the kitchen table, because knowing her dad, this would probably take a while.

—The End—

Thank you for reading FALLING FAST. I really hope you enjoyed it and that you'll consider leaving a review at one of your favorite online retailers. It's a great way to help other readers discover new books.

If you liked FALLING FAST and would like to read more, turn the page for a list of my other books. And if you don't want to miss any future releases, please feel free to join my newsletter:

http://kayleacross.com/v2/newsletter/

Complete Booklist

ROMANTIC SUSPENSE

DEA FAST Series
Falling Fast

Colebrook Siblings Trilogy
Brody's Vow
Wyatt's Stand
Easton's Claim

Hostage Rescue Team Series
Marked
Targeted
Hunted
Disavowed
Avenged
Exposed
Seized
Wanted
Betrayed
Reclaimed

Titanium Security Series
Ignited
Singed
Burned
Extinguished
Rekindled
Blindsided: A Titanium Christmas novella

Bagram Special Ops Series
Deadly Descent
Tactical Strike

Lethal Pursuit
Danger Close
Collateral Damage
Never Surrender (a MacKenzie Family novella)

Suspense Series
Out of Her League
Cover of Darkness
No Turning Back
Relentless
Absolution

PARANORMAL ROMANCE
Empowered Series
Darkest Caress

HISTORICAL ROMANCE
The Vacant Chair

EROTIC ROMANCE (writing as *Callie Croix*)
Deacon's Touch
Dillon's Claim
No Holds Barred
Touch Me
Let Me In
Covert Seduction

Acknowledgements

As always, a big thank you to my behind-the-scenes team in helping me get this story ready for the world. So excited to launch this new series!

About the Author

NY Times and USA Today Bestselling author Kaylea Cross writes edge-of-your-seat military romantic suspense. Her work has won many awards and has been nominated for both the Daphne du Maurier and the National Readers' Choice Awards. A Registered Massage Therapist by trade, Kaylea is also an avid gardener, artist, Civil War buff, Special Ops aficionado, belly dance enthusiast and former nationally-carded softball pitcher. She lives in Vancouver, BC with her husband and family.

You can visit Kaylea at www.kayleacross.com. If you would like to be notified of future releases, please join her newsletter: http://kayleacross.com/v2/newsletter/

CPSIA information can be obtained
at www.ICGtesting.com
Printed in the USA
LVOW08s1630240417
531982LV00003B/751/P